GRANDPA'S WISH

Melanie is growing tired of her job at a family law firm, until she is tasked with tracing a Mr Davies, the beneficiary of a late client's estate. Tracking him down, Melanie is surprised to find Robbie-Joe uninterested in the terms of the will, especially when he learns that it belonged to a grandfather he had no idea existed. To claim his fortune, Robbie-Joe must complete twelve challenges in twelve months. But Melanie has a challenge of her own: to stop her feelings for Robbie-Joe becoming anything more than professional . . .

Books by Sarah Swatridge
in the Linford Romance Library:

AN HONOURABLE WAGER

We hope you enjoy this book.
Please return or renew it by the due date.
You can renew it at **www.norfolk.gov.uk/libraries**
or by using our free library app. Otherwise you can
phone **0344 800 8020** - please have your library
card and pin ready.
You can sign up for email reminders too.

LST:LP1

NORFOLK COUNTY COUNCIL
LIBRARY AND INFORMATION SERVICE

SARAH SWATRIDGE

GRANDPA'S WISH

Complete and Unabridged

LINFORD
Leicester

First published in Great Britain in 2018

First Linford Edition
published 2020

A catalogue record for this book is available
from the British Library.

ISBN 978–1–4448–4361–3

Grandpa's Wish

'Am I in the wrong job?' Melanie asked Miss McCree one evening.

'What on earth makes you say that, dear?'

'Don't say anything at work, will you?' Melanie continued. 'It's just that the job isn't as interesting as I thought it would be.'

'You haven't been with the firm very long,' Anita McCree pointed out.

She herself had been with Darcy and Darcy Solicitors for nearly forty years.

'I'm sure it will get better as you get more experienced, Melanie.'

'I'll only improve if they ever let me get involved in anything more interesting than a house conveyance!'

'You've got to start somewhere,' Anita told her.

'I have a law degree. It's not as though I'm some work experience girl.'

1

'Don't underestimate conveyancing. It's very important that you get it right for the people buying and selling their homes.'

'I realise that.' Melanie yawned. 'But it's so boring.'

'I wouldn't be surprised if Mr Darcy has set you this task so he can see how seriously you take it. He'll want to know how committed you are.'

'I suppose so,' Melanie agreed. 'Shall I put the kettle on?'

Secretly, Melanie feared she could be stuck in a rut and still working for Darcy and Darcy until she retired.

'A cup of tea would be lovely. Will you join me in the lounge?'

Melanie Harper lodged with Anita McCree. She rented her spare bedroom and Melanie had lived with her for the last six months since leaving university and starting with the small, family law firm.

As Melanie waited for the kettle to boil she wondered if she'd ever be able to admit to the serious Miss McCree that the main reason she'd applied to this particular law firm was because she was intrigued to meet not one, but two Mr Darcys.

It soon became perfectly clear that neither of them resembled the hunky Fitzwilliam Darcy from Jane Austen's 'Pride And Prejudice'.

The Darcy brothers, were of medium height with greying hair and a stoop. They weren't twins but they did look alike and it had taken Melanie a while to sort out which one was David, who generally handled matrimonial cases, and which Peter, who did everything else.

Darcy and Darcy Solicitors were not known for taking on new staff. They had never even considered the future of the company or actively encouraged new business. There had always been a steady flow of trade and neither of the Darcy brothers had extravagant tastes.

David Darcy, despite spending his time working with people whose relationships were going through a bad patch, had married Eva, an artist, when they were both very young and still lived very happily with Mrs Darcy who, Melanie thought, resembled a sparrow.

Peter Darcy remained a bachelor.

As far as Melanie could tell, all he ever did was work or read. He was an avid reader of crime fiction.

★　★　★

The following morning at work Anita beamed over at Melanie from her large wooden desk.

'What's got into you?' Melanie asked. 'Have you told them you're taking early retirement?'

'Nothing of the sort! Unlike you, I love my job here and I've no plans yet to give up.'

'So what is it?'

'Mr Darcy — Mr Peter, that is — would like you to trace a gentleman called Davies in connection with a Mr Huntley's estate. I believe this Mr Davies is a beneficiary.'

'Am I allowed to tell him?' Melanie asked, mindful that Mr Darcy was probably testing her out and that she always had to be careful how much she was allowed to say.

'You can tell him that he's a beneficiary, but no further details. He's required to come to the office and listen to the terms of the will.'

Melanie spent the rest of the morning on the case. By lunchtime she was feeling despondent.

'There's not much to go on,' she complained. 'The address we have is out of date, it doesn't even exist any more. In fact there's a whole new housing estate built there and there are hundreds of Davies around.'

'You wanted something more interesting to do,' Miss McCree reminded her. 'I hope you're not going to give up at the first hurdle.'

'Of course not,' Melanie told her, although she was running out of places to try. 'I'm going to go and get a sandwich. Do you want anything?'

'I'll have a cup of tea when you get back and perhaps we can take a look at what you've tried so far?'

The walk to the corner shop and lunch revived Melanie so that she was ready to track down the elusive Mr Davies.

'I've looked on LinkedIn and Facebook. There were two R.J. Davies from this area. I've spoken to them both but neither originally lived at Stanlake Farm.'

'Stanlake Farm?' Miss McCree repeated. 'What's the date of the will?'

'It was originally written in 1970 but a codicil was added in 1988 and that names Robert Joseph Davies who lived at Stanlake Farm at that time.'

'I can't remember a farm by that name.' Anita McCree frowned. 'And I have lived here all my life.'

'That's probably because it was a mobile home park until it burned down in the early nineties.'

'Oh, yes, that's right. There was a dreadful fire and the council had to relocate everyone. That is going to make it rather difficult.'

'I've been on to the council. It's just a long shot, but I was thinking, if it was a gypsy caravan site, then maybe there would be a record of which site they were moved to.'

'Good thinking, but don't Romanies roam around?' Anita asked. 'Surely they could be anywhere by now.'

'True, but I have spoken with the Traveller Education department and there is still a large family called Davies who are in the area. Of course, R.J. Davies may not be amongst them, but I'm betting they're related.'

'Good work.'

'I'm going to visit the site first thing in the morning, so wish me luck.'

First Impressions

Melanie was met with suspicious looks when she arrived at the trailer park the following morning.

'Excuse me?' she called. 'I'm looking for a Robert Joseph Davies. Is he here?'

At first she was ignored, then a dog started barking and a man came out to see what had set it off.

'What do you want?' the man asked. His voice was gruff.

'I'm looking for Robert Davies. I need to give him an urgent message.'

'You can give it to me,' the man said.

'Are you Robert Joseph Davies?' Melanie asked as she felt in her pocket for a business card.

'What's it about?'

'I've got to give the message to him personally, but I can say I think it will be to his advantage.'

'You'd better come in and see Queenie.'

The man led Melanie into the kitchen area of a long cream mobile home with lacy curtains and plastic flowers in the window. It was spotlessly clean.

'Wait here,' the man told her but a few minutes later he returned and beckoned her into another room. Melanie wished now she'd posted a formal letter, but at least she'd told Miss McCree exactly where she was and knew there would be a search party sent out if she didn't arrive at work within the hour.

'Robbie-Joe is my grandson,' an elderly lady dressed in black said. 'What do you want with him?'

The woman sat, fully dressed, on the edge of her bed. She reminded Melanie of a Victorian ghost as she was dressed in a long dark skirt and black blouse with lace cuffs.

'I work for Darcy and Darcy Solicitors. A Robert Joseph Davies has been named in a will as a beneficiary and I'm trying to track him down. Did he used to live at the old Stanlake Farm site?'

'We all did.' The woman nodded.

'Here's my card,' Melanie said. 'Would you ask him to contact the office so we can check whether he's the person we're looking for?'

'Would this have anything to do with Robert Huntley?' she asked.

'I really can't say. Just ask your grandson to get in touch, please. I can't stress how important it is for him.'

When Melanie returned to the office and explained that she'd left a message and her card with Mr Davies's grandmother, Anita congratulated her.

'I'm glad you didn't give up. I thought you were going to at one point but you persevered, and that's important. It wasn't an easy thing to do but you used your initiative and it looks like you might have been successful.'

Melanie smiled at Miss McCree and hoped that this grandson would actually turn up. She wasn't 100 percent sure that the message would be passed on, or the invitation taken up.

Just as Melanie and Miss McCree

were packing up to go home that evening, there was a knock on the office door.

A giant of a man stood in the doorway blocking out the light. He had black curly hair and the most enormous hands.

'I'm Robbie-Joe,' he announced. 'Queenie said I was to see you.'

★   ★   ★

Peter Darcy was taller than his brother but even he was dwarfed by Robbie-Joe who seemed to fill the office with his presence.

'Please sit down.' Mr Darcy gestured to a nearby chair. 'Miss Harper, you'd better stay and take notes.'

Melanie shot him a look as if to say she was a trainee lawyer and not his secretary. Just because Miss McCree had to leave promptly this evening, it didn't mean she had to step in.

'I do have . . . '

'Please, Miss Harper. This won't take

11

long and then you can finish whatever it was you were working on.'

'Fine,' Melanie said, sitting down opposite Robbie-Joe.

'Firstly, you'll understand, we have to verify you are the correct Mr Robert Joseph Davies who resided at Stanlake Farm? Can you produce evidence of this?'

'I left there when I was about two. There was a fire — my parents were both killed. I don't remember the place at all but Queenie, my grandmother, said that's where we'd lived.'

'And can you prove this?'

'I can bring her in,' the man said. His voice was deep with a sing-song rhythm to it. 'In fact you'd have to come to her. She'd never set foot in a place like this,' he told them as a matter of fact.

Melanie watched as Mr Darcy's eyes widened. Nobody told Mr Darcy what he had to do.

'I think I can ascertain whether or not this is the correct gentleman,' Melanie said as she picked up a buff-coloured folder which contained all her research so far.

She produced a photocopy of a newspaper cutting and handed it to Mr Darcy.

'It clearly says that baby Robbie-Joe was rescued from the fire but suffered burns to his left arm. I have it on good authority that, although the burn will have healed, the scar will still be visible.'

Robbie-Joe looked confused but began to roll up his left shirt sleeve to reveal a red patch of skin where the hairs refused to grow.

'Is this what you mean?' he asked.

'Well done, Miss Harper. I think we've found our man,' Mr Darcy said with obvious relief. 'Now, let's get down to business.'

Mr Darcy briefly glanced at the clock. He was a creature of habit and in the time Melanie had worked for the firm she had not known him or his brother work later than five-thirty.

However, he opened a large box file and withdrew the last will and testament of Robert Huntley.

As he began to slowly read the formal jargon in his monotonous voice, Melanie watched as Robbie-Joe's eyes glazed over. Even she, with her law degree, was struggling to keep awake.

'Perhaps, Mr Darcy,' Melanie began, hoping she'd be forgiven for interrupting, 'as it's late in the day, could you just highlight the main points, and we can make a copy for Mr Davies to read at his leisure?'

'I suppose I could, if that would be acceptable, Mr Davies?'

Their visitor nodded.

'Basically, Mr Huntley died recently and has left a considerable sum of money and property to you, but . . . ' Mr Darcy paused and looked up, waiting for Robbie-Joe to make eye contact. 'There are a number of challenges Mr Huntley has stipulated that you complete to my satisfaction, before we can release the capital.'

'I don't understand.' Robbie-Joe frowned. 'Why would a complete stranger leave money to me?'

'Ah,' Mr Darcy said, fiddling with the collar of his crisp white shirt. He always did this when he wasn't happy about something. 'It appears Mr Huntley believes you are his grandson and his only heir.'

Robbie-Joe sat there looking puzzled and then he scratched his head.

'Queenie and Grandpa Joe are the only grandparents I know. Maybe I'm not the man you were looking for, after all.'

'But your arm . . . ' Melanie reminded him.

'I'll get Miss Harper to make you a copy and you can read the rest for yourself. Then, should you have any queries, you can make an appointment and we can discuss the matter. Is that acceptable to you?'

'Yes,' their visitor agreed although Melanie thought he didn't sound very sure. He followed her out into the reception area and waited patiently for her to copy the document.

'Oh, typical,' Melanie said after refilling the machine with paper. 'Now it's run out of ink.'

'I'm not in any hurry.'

'It's going to take me a few minutes,' Melanie admitted. 'Can I get you a cup of tea or coffee while you wait?'

'A mug of tea would be great, if it's no trouble. I can call back tomorrow if you need to go.'

'Fortunately I'm not in any hurry this evening,' Melanie told him.

She walked over to the kettle and filled it up, only to find they were completely out of milk.

'Do you take milk?' she asked.

Typically he nodded.

'I'm really sorry but . . . ' she began as she waved the empty carton at him.

Just at that moment Mr Darcy appeared with his coat and briefcase.

'You still here?' he said in surprise. 'What's the problem?'

'No problem,' Robbie-Joe said, picking up a white envelope. 'I was just leaving. Thank you, Miss Harper,' he added and followed Mr Darcy out of the door clutching his empty envelope.

★ ★ ★

Ten minutes later there was a little tap on the office door and Robbie-Joe popped his head round, giving her a lop-sided smile.

'Is the coast clear?' he asked.

'I've done your copy,' Melanie said, handing him a second white envelope. 'Thank you for not dropping me in it.'

'I think you owe me.'

'Well . . . '

'I'm not hot on all this legal stuff. How about we go over the road to the café and I'll buy us a drink and you can tell me what it's all about?'

'Do you really want to discuss it in a public place?'

'It's almost empty. They'll be closing soon.'

'Well, if you're sure,' Melanie said as she locked up her desk and switched off the lights.

A Brief Rendezvous

'So, basically you're telling me,' Robbie-Joe said half an hour later, 'that this guy who thinks he's my grandad has left me loads of money if I complete twelve tasks?'

'That just about sums it up. You have a year to complete the challenges and you have to provide suitable evidence for each one you've achieved. I think they have to be done in order and you'll only know what they are once you've finished the previous one, so you can't plan ahead.'

Robbie-Joe finished his tea and stood up.

'Thanks for explaining it, but no thanks.'

'What do you mean, no thanks?'

'I don't want it.'

'But it's your grandfather's will,' Melanie said. 'He wants you to have his money and he's got no-one else to leave it to.'

'So why make me work for it?'

'I don't know. I'd have thought you would know your own grandpa.'

'I must be off,' Robbie-Joe said, bowing his head. 'It's been nice meeting you.'

'Here, wait,' Melanie called, waving the papers at him. 'Don't forget these.'

'I told you, I don't want them.' And with that, he was gone.

Melanie wasn't sure if she should have returned to the office and placed the copy of the will inside the safe rather than taking it home with her on the bus.

Later that evening she discussed the matter with a reluctant Anita.

'There's confidential information contained in that envelope. It was meant for your client.'

'I explained what happened. He left without taking it. I couldn't leave it in the café, could I?'

'Of course not.'

'I had intended to post it off to him tomorrow but, to be honest, I think he'll just put it in the bin.'

'I suppose that is his decision,' Anita said thoughtfully. 'We can't force him to accept the challenge.'

'I know we agreed we wouldn't discuss work at home, and I'm sorry for bringing it up, but I don't know what to do.'

'As it happens, I do know that Peter Darcy is out of the office first thing tomorrow morning,' Anita confided. 'So why don't you call round to see Mr Davies at his home on your way to work and leave the envelope with him? I'm sure, once he's slept on it, he'll be very pleased that you did.'

'That's what I was hoping you'd say,' Melanie admitted. 'I'll leave early and drop it off as quickly as I can, then get to the office. Hopefully I'll be there before Mr Darcy arrives.'

'Good,' Anita said, 'and from then on can we go by the book? There are rules and protocol to be followed and you need to learn to do that.'

'I do understand.'

'I know you do, and that's why, just this once, I'll help you out, but you're not to make a habit of doing things your own way. Is that clear?'

'Absolutely.'

★ ★ ★

Melanie arrived just as a white van was leaving the plot. It occurred to her that she might have missed Robbie-Joe but, if that was the case, there was nothing she could do about it.

At first she wondered why there was nobody about. The site was made up of several mobile homes but it appeared to be a ghost town.

She stood, holding the envelope, wondering what she ought to do next when she became aware of a face at the window. It was Queenie, Robbie-Joe's grandmother.

Without waiting to be invited in, Melanie marched up to the trailer and knocked.

'Hello?' she called. 'I'm really sorry to bother you . . . '

'I passed on your message,' Queenie said.

'Yes. Thank you — but when he came to the office yesterday, he forgot this envelope,' Melanie explained as she stretched the truth. 'If I leave it here will you make sure he gets it, and reads it?'

'I'll give it to him when he comes home for tea,' Queenie said. 'You can trust me.'

'You will make sure he reads it?'

'I can't promise you that, but I will speak to him.'

'You'll speak to him about what?' a man's deep voice said.

Melanie saw Queenie recoil before she turned to see the same man who'd let her in the other day. He didn't look pleased to see her.

'Stay!' he said to the dog. Then he walked over and picked up the envelope.

Melanie was about to tell him it was

addressed to Robbie-Joe but there was no need. He thrust it back at Melanie.

'He'd have taken it when you first offered it to him, if he wanted it,' the strange man said. 'Now go.'

'But he needs to read it,' Melanie argued. 'I don't think you understand how important it is.' She looked at Queenie.

'And you don't seem to know when you're not welcome,' the man said and, as if the dog had understood every word, he growled.

'OK, I'll go,' Melanie said, accepting the envelope. 'You can tell him I'll be in the café tonight if he changes his mind.'

★ ★ ★

Back in the office, Melanie worked hard to catch up with her conveyancing work which she'd neglected a little recently while she'd been trying to track down the elusive Mr Davies.

'I doubt if he'll come back,' Anita said.

'Pardon?'

'I appreciate that you've worked really hard to get on top of things today but every time the door opens or the phone rings you look up and then look away as if you're disappointed.'

'I just want to hand over the envelope to him, that's all.'

'He was quite a handsome man, in a rugged sort of way.'

'That's got absolutely nothing to do with it,' Melanie said quickly but she could feel herself blushing.

Melanie Shares Her Secret

They'd been sitting in the café chatting for half an hour and Robbie-Joe hadn't even opened the envelope.

'Why?' he said again. 'Why would a stranger leave me anything?'

'This Robert Huntley obviously believes you're his grandson. You are called Robert, too, or is that just a coincidence?'

'Lots of people are called Robert. Are you named after anyone?'

Melanie froze for a moment as she considered his question. After a moment's hesitation she came to her senses and focused the conversation back to her client.

'We're not talking about me. I haven't been left a huge fortune. You have — and whether you think this chap has any-thing to do with you or not, you've got nothing to lose by listening to what he's offering.'

'What's in it for you?'

'Me?'

'Yes. Do you get a percentage?'

'No. Of course not. It's just my job to find you as you were named as a beneficiary in Mr Huntley's will. I don't get anything out of it.'

'So why are you here?'

Melanie glanced at the clock. It was almost six and officially she finished at five-thirty. Why was she here?

'Just take the information home and read it through and, as Mr Darcy says, if you have any questions then come and chat to him about it.'

'Will I have questions?'

'Well, as I told you, it's quite an unusual sort of will. Rather than just leaving you the money, he's set up a series of challenges which you have to do in order to earn the money as it were. I think Mr Darcy will have to give you a challenge one at a time.'

'So he didn't really want to give it to me?' Robbie-Joe argued. 'What sort of grandfather is that?'

'I'm sure he had his reasons.'

'If he was a real grandpa, he'd have been in touch before now. The only grandparents I've ever known are Queenie and Grandpa Joe. No-one else.'

'Are they your mother's parents or your father's?'

'We're all one big family,' he told her as if he was avoiding her question.

'You are so lucky,' Melanie said without thinking.

'Lucky?'

'To have such a close family.'

'Isn't yours like that?'

'I'm adopted.' Melanie wondered why she was telling a complete stranger these personal details about herself.

'I suppose I'm adopted, too,' Robbie-Joe said with a smile. 'That fire you told the old man about, it killed both my parents. Queenie adopted me after that and brought me up as her own son, even though I'm really her grandson.'

'You're still her flesh and blood,' Melanie said. 'And I bet you're surrounded by cousins and other family members.'

'I do have lots of cousins,' Robbie-Joe admitted. He looked down at the table.

Melanie thought he looked suddenly sad but, just as she was wondering how to cheer him up, he glanced up and looked into her eyes.

'Maybe you have lots of cousins, too, you just haven't met them yet.'

'Maybe I do,' Melanie agreed. 'But we're talking about your family and not mine.'

'Actually, we were talking about both our backgrounds.'

'But it's yours we're meant to be focusing on. Do give some serious thought to what Mr Darcy told you.'

'Why is it so important to you?' Robbie-Joe asked. 'That is, if you've told me the truth and you really don't gain anything by it.'

'Of course I've told you the truth,' Melanie snapped. 'Why would I lie?'

Robbie-Joe covered one of her dainty hands with his large palm.

'I didn't mean to upset you,' he told her. 'But surely you can see why I am suspicious?'

'I suppose so,' Melanie agreed. 'Just read the will and make your own decision. I've probably said too much already.'

'You definitely haven't said too much,' Robbie-Joe said with a grin. 'You haven't told me how I can contact you again.'

Melanie was confused for a moment. It seemed absolutely obvious to her that all he had to do was to contact Darcy and Darcy Solicitors again and no doubt she would answer the phone.

It was only when she looked up at Robbie-Joe and saw the smile on his face that she realised he was flirting with her.

'Please don't get the wrong idea,' she said quickly. 'It's just that it took me so long to find you and you could be giving up a small fortune. I'd hate to think that one day in the future you'd look back and regret your decision.'

Robbie-Joe smiled at her and Melanie realised his warm hand still covered hers.

'You're right,' Robbie-Joe said, gazing into her eyes and making her feel a little off balance. 'I might regret it if I don't come back into your office.'

'Let's keep this strictly professional,' Melanie said, standing up as tall as her five foot two inches would allow and removing her hand from the table. 'I should never have told you about myself. I shouldn't have joined you here, either. I should have posted off a photocopy and left it at that.'

'But you didn't.'

'I'm new to this, as you've probably guessed and, as you can tell, I've got a lot to learn. I don't think Mr Darcy really wanted to take me on in the first place but somehow Anita, his secretary, persuaded him. I don't want to let her down so I have to prove myself to Mr Darcy.'

'The only person you have to prove yourself to,' Robbie-Joe said, 'is yourself, but I can see why you feel the way you do.'

'Sorry, you two love birds,' the café owner said, 'but we're closing. You'll have to carry on your date somewhere else.'

'It's not a date,' Melanie said quickly.

She picked up the large envelope and held it out for Robbie-Joe to take.

'It's of no use to me.'

'How do you know until you've read it?'

'I don't know. And as I'm not great at reading, I suppose I'll never know.'

The Dilemma

'So,' Melanie said to Anita over coffee later that evening, 'should I speak to Mr Darcy about it or just offer to read it out to our client?'

'This client that you've already met twice for coffee?' Anita McCree teased. 'The one with the lovely eyes?'

'It was tea, actually.'

'You know what I'm going to say.' Anita smiled. 'Speak to Mr Darcy. Maybe he'll suggest you go through it with the client. You might not believe it, but I'm sure Peter is as keen as you are that Mr Davies gets his inheritance in the end.'

'OK, I'll do as you say and speak to Mr Darcy in the morning. Is everything like this? I mean I thought reading a will would be so straightforward and easy.'

'Most of them are,' Anita told her,

'but this is an interesting one, don't you think? And you did want something to get your teeth into, didn't you?'

The following morning Melanie took Peter Darcy his first cup of coffee of the day and explained the situation to him.

'I could read it to him, if you like,' she offered.

'You could, but I'm not sure he'd agree.'

'Surely it's worth a try. I'd hate him to miss out on such an opportunity as this.'

'I must admit I suspected we'd have a bit of a battle over this one,' Peter Darcy admitted as he sipped his strong black coffee.

'What will happen to the money if Mr Davies doesn't claim it?'

'There is a Plan B in place, but let's hope we don't need it. I'm happy to leave it with you to make arrangements with Mr Davies so you can read it to him.

'You'll have to make it clear that he will have to come in here approximately once a month to give evidence that he's completed the first task and to accept the next one. He only has a year to do it and who knows, they may get more complicated.'

'Is that a year from now or when he accepts the challenge?'

'A year from the date he's given the first one. I don't suppose it will be easy, so don't you go making him any promises. His grandfather wants him to work for his money.'

'Why is that?' Melanie asked.

'You, young lady, ask too many questions. Now, I'm sure I'm paying you good money to be working, not interrogating me. Be off with you!'

Melanie scooped up the file and left the office. She wasn't sure if Mr Darcy was teasing her or if he was deadly serious. The good news was that she had the ideal excuse to contact Robbie-Joe again.

Easier said than done.

Melanie's only contact details for Robbie-Joe were via Queenie, his grandmother. As much as she hated the thought of visiting the traveller site again, she couldn't see any other way around it.

She had no phone number and, if what he said was true, if he really couldn't read, then there was no point sending him a letter.

'I've been thinking,' Melanie told Anita at lunchtime. 'Maybe if I go back to see Queenie during the day then the other man, the scary one, won't be around and perhaps she can tell me when Robbie-Joe gets home from work or even give me his mobile number.'

'Do you think she's on your side?' Anita asked as she bit into her sandwich.

'I really don't know, but she did pass on the message to him and he did come into the office. Actually, I think she's my only hope.'

'Perhaps you could slip out after lunch,' Anita agreed. 'But only for an hour, mind. There's still a lot to be done and I know you've got lots of phone calls to return this afternoon.'

'I know, but thanks.'

★　★　★

Melanie took a deep breath as she approached the trailer site. Once again it was quiet.

A dog was sleeping outside one of the mobile homes. Washing hung outside a few of the others.

Further along, a couple of small children played while their mothers sat on the steps and chatted.

As she looked around, she noticed lots of black bin bags lying around. It must be the rubbish collection day, she thought, but then remembered the bags had been there on her previous visits.

She knocked on Queenie's door and stood back just in case the dog was about. There was no reply but Melanie was sure someone was inside.

'Queenie?' she called. 'It's only me, Melanie, Robbie-Joe's friend.'

Still there was no response but

Melanie did not want to leave without successfully having tracked him down.

She tried the door. It opened.

'Queenie?' she called again.

This time she definitely heard a sound coming from her bedroom.

'I just need a quick word.'

'Come in,' Queenie said.

Her voice was stronger than Melanie had been expecting.

'I'm so sorry to bother you again,' Melanie began. 'I don't know what Robbie-Joe's told you but I've been given permission to read through the will with him and explain it all. I think that would be helpful. Perhaps you could ask him to call in to the office again? Or if I could have his mobile number?'

'I'll tell him.'

Melanie sensed their meeting was at an end. She had made her request and Queenie had agreed to pass on the message, as she had done before.

She turned to go, wondering if that was going to be the best she could do.

'You have such a lovely home here,' Melanie said. Her eyes rested on a vase of spring flowers. 'I love daffodils.'

'They're from Robbie-Joe. He's a good lad. I don't want to lose him.'

'I'm not trying to take him away. No-one is trying to do that,' Melanie said, turning back and looking Queenie in the eyes.

'Think about it,' was all she added.

She left Queenie's home but didn't leave the site straight away. Once again she noticed the rubbish.

'You from the council?' one of the women asked.

'No,' Melanie said. 'Is there a problem here?'

'They don't collect it. I bet you have your rubbish collected, don't you?'

'I could phone the council on your behalf,' Melanie said. 'You'll get rats if it's left much longer.'

They both glanced at the children kicking a ball around. Melanie's mind was made up.

'Here's my card. I'll phone the

council this afternoon. All the rubbish needs to be near the entrance so it's easy to collect. My name's Melanie Harper, what's yours?'

'None of your business,'

'OK. I'll let Queenie know if there's any problem.'

'You know Queenie?' the woman asked. Melanie nodded.

'You police? Is Robbie-Joe OK?'

'I'm not the police and Robbie-Joe is fine, as far as I know, so don't worry.'

Melanie left the site and then hurried back to the office. She spent the afternoon chasing up estate agents and calling clients to update them on the sale of their properties.

She also tracked down the right person in the council and mentioned to them the health risk to the children and families if the rubbish was not collected from the traveller site.

'Thank you,' she said when the manager agreed to have it collected first thing the following morning. 'And will it be collected on a regular basis?'

'It has to be bagged up. My men haven't got time to go litter picking.'

'If it's all in bags near the entrance will you collect it each week, say, every Thursday morning?' Melanie asked assertively. 'It's getting to the stage when it's becoming quite a health risk and I'm sure the council wouldn't want that. There are small children living on the site.'

'OK. I'll add them to the Thursday round, but it does need to be ready for us to collect. Understand?'

'I'll make that perfectly clear,' Melanie agreed.

Despite her forceful words, her heart was pounding nervously by the time she finished the call.

A Welcome Surprise

Melanie was filing away the last few papers at the end of the day, when the front door creaked open. Once again Robbie-Joe's large frame filled the doorway.

He was wearing a dark jacket but in his hands he carried a small posy of tête-à-tête daffodils.

'Mr Davies,' Anita said, rising from her desk, 'our opening hours are nine until five-thirty, our last appointment being four-thirty. Do you understand?'

'I do, miss, but I had a message from my grandmother that I was to call in again to see Miss . . . ' He looked in Melanie's direction.

'Miss Harper is very busy.'

'No problem, Miss McCree, I've just finished my filing. Now, Mr Davies, do come and sit down and I'll explain why I wanted to see you.'

Melanie gestured to a chair. Robbie-Joe sat, still clutching the flowers.

'Can I get you a drink?' Melanie asked, as she would any client visiting the office.

Today he shook his head, but did sit down.

Melanie leaned across her desk and spoke in a low voice even though Anita was busy tidying her own desk at the other side of the room.

'I explained the situation to Mr Darcy,' she began, 'and he's given me his permission to read and to go through the will with you, bit by bit, so that you understand. It will take some time, so we'd probably better arrange for you to come in another day.'

'I've already told you,' he said. 'I'm not interested.'

'So, why have you come in again?'

'I thought you wanted to see me,' he said and looked down at the flowers, 'and to bring you these.'

He handed over the daffodils.

'Oh, they're lovely.' Melanie gasped as if she had only just noticed them.

'Let me put them in water.'

Melanie rushed to the little kitchen area and tried to fill a glass with water but she'd switched the tap on too much and it sprayed everywhere. It took her a few moments to dry herself off and then to arrange the little yellow flowers in the makeshift vase.

When she returned to her desk, the chair was empty and there was no sign of Robbie-Joe.

'He's gone,' Anita said.

Melanie sighed and her shoulders dropped. For some reason she felt disappointed by his sudden disappearance.

Carefully she arranged the flowers on her desk and finished locking things away at the end of the day.

'Are you visiting your mother tonight?' Anita asked.

Melanie nodded.

'I won't be late but I'll have tea with Mum. See you later.'

Outside the office was a large white van with writing on the side. *Joe the Gardener.* Underneath was a mobile number.

Melanie wasn't certain, but she was pretty sure it was the same white van that had left the trailer site just as she had arrived the other morning.

She got out her phone and took a picture of the van and zoomed in on the phone number. She could always delete it if it wasn't his vehicle.

She said a fond farewell to Anita and they went their separate ways. Melanie glanced over at the café opposite and saw the unmistakable frame of Robbie-Joe.

He waved and her heart did a little flip, while the voice in her head told her to keep her distance, keep everything very professional.

Melanie returned his wave but carried on along the road. She hadn't gone far before she heard footsteps behind her. Someone was running.

She turned to find the huge frame of Robbie-Joe as he caught her up.

'You didn't come in the café,' he accused.

'I told you before. We have to keep

this professional. Anita's just told you the last appointment is four-thirty each day. You just walked out.'

'I thought we could have a drink and maybe I could take you out for a meal and you can read that document to me.'

'I'm sorry. That's not the way it works.'

'I thought you liked me,' Robbie-Joe said.

Under the street light she caught the look in his large blue eyes. He looked sad.

'If you come in earlier tomorrow or another day then we can read through the will in the office and you can ask any questions and I can tell you what your first task will be — the first thing your grandfather wanted you to do.'

'But I work until it gets dark. I don't get paid unless I work and if I don't get paid I can't buy food for Queenie.' Robbie-Joe explained.

'Do you work full time?' she asked.

He nodded.

'I work during daylight hours. But it's

hard when it rains heavily. I could come in then.'

'That's all very well, but you are not my only client, and I may have a meeting with someone else.'

'Do you have a meeting now?' he asked.

'As it happens, I do. I need to do some grocery shopping and take it to my mother.'

'Is that your real mother?'

The question took Melanie back. She knew from a young age she'd been adopted, but her adoptive parents were very kind and loving and she had never, not once, questioned that they were not her real mum and dad.

She cursed herself for sharing her personal story with a stranger. It had unnerved her and, she admitted, made her face the fact that somewhere in the back of her mind, she had started to wonder.

She stopped and looked up at him.

'If I did make time to read you the will, are you ready to accept it and carry out the tasks he's set you? I don't want to waste your time, and mine.'

'I have thought about it. I can't guarantee I'll go through with it when I hear what I have to do, but at least I will listen. And that's the honest truth.'

Melanie took a deep breath. She knew she had to make a decision, and he had been honest with her for which she was grateful.

'OK. Come into the office tomorrow or Friday after work, but as early as you can and we'll make a start. If necessary we can finish over in the café, if you are absolutely sure you don't mind discussing this in such a public place.'

'The forecast is not good for tomorrow afternoon so I will come and find you.'

'Great. That's settled then.'

'It's a date,' Robbie-Joe said with a grin as he turned and headed off in the opposite direction.

'Not a date, an appointment,' Melanie called but he didn't seem to hear.

★　★　★

That night Melanie struggled to get to sleep. She thought of Anita McCree who often said she couldn't sleep and would frequently get up in the middle of the night and make herself tea and toast.

Melanie had never had such problems . . . until now.

She closed her eyes and tried to get comfortable. She was warm and cosy but there was so much on her mind.

Firstly there was June Harper, her mother. The lovely, kind and caring woman who had brought her up and welcomed her into her home along with Brian Harper.

Melanie had a happy childhood and had never questioned the fact that perhaps they weren't really her parents, because they did as much for her — and more — as everyone else's parents did.

However, tonight when she'd been making tea and doing a bit of cleaning for June, who wasn't as mobile as she used to be, Melanie had been aware that they didn't really look at all alike.

For the first time she'd wanted to ask about her birth mother. She wondered if there were any photographs.

And she wondered why she'd been adopted in the first place.

Melanie drifted into a semi sleep and dozed for a couple of hours before waking at one o'clock. There had been something her mother was trying to tell her, only it wasn't her mother, it had been Queenie.

Now she was awake she lay curled up in her warm bed and went through the conversation she'd had with Queenie recently. What was it she'd said that had stuck in Melanie's mind?

Eventually she recalled how anxious Queenie was. She'd been frightened of losing her grandson, and now it hit her. If Robbie-Joe did inherit a property and a large amount of money then would he continue to live in a caravan?

If it had been anyone else she would instantly expect them to sell the caravan and buy a house, maybe even one for Queenie and one for himself.

But Robbie-Joe was not like anyone else she had ever met. He came from a travelling background and she wondered if he would actually want to leave all his family and friends who lived on the caravan site.

She saw now why Queenie had been so worried.

It could cause all sorts of problems for Robbie-Joe because he'd not necessarily belong with his cousins at the trailer park, nor might he be happy and settled in a traditional house.

She could see the dilemma and wondered whether Queenie had said anything to him.

Once Melanie had begun to understand Queenie's fears she was able to settle down to sleep, but when she awoke she was trying to see the features of a woman. She was just a silhouette, not dissimilar to Anita McCree her landlady, but somehow not familiar at all.

The stranger, she knew, was her real mother.

The First Challenge

As Robbie-Joe had predicted, the weather deteriorated as the day went on and at four o'clock a rather wet figure entered the office. He shook himself dry as Anita got him to take off his coat and hang it up.

Once again he was carrying a small bunch of spring flowers, but this time it was a mixture of colours.

'You really don't need to bring me flowers every time you see me,' Melanie said, 'although they are lovely and I do love fresh flowers.'

'Those were from me,' Robbie-Joe said, pointing at the daffodils in the glass of water. 'These are from my grandmother.'

'Queenie?'

'You spoke to the council.'

'Oh, great,' Melanie said. 'They collected the rubbish then? Good. You must tell Queenie and everyone else the council will come on a Thursday but the rubbish must all be bagged up and left near the site entrance so it's easy for the men to collect. Can you spread the word?'

'Of course.' He smiled. 'Is that my first task?'

Melanie chuckled. He had a lovely open smile. She suspected that you got what you saw with Robbie-Joe. You could take him or leave him; he wasn't out to impress.

'Right, let's make a start,' Melanie said, tearing herself away from his smile.

Once Melanie had read aloud the will to Robbie-Joe, she told him of his first challenge.

'Oh, this is an easy one.' She laughed as she read it for the first time. 'Remember you have only one year from now to complete all twelve tasks. So that's roughly one a month, but I suppose some may take longer than others to complete.'

'Go on.'

'You have to show Mr Darcy a certificate with your name on. That shouldn't be too difficult.' Robbie-Joe looked blank. 'Oh, come on, you must have a school certificate, a qualification or something to do with your gardening business? Even your birth certificate would do.'

'I have an accountant who deals with all my paperwork. I don't think I've anything.'

'But you must have your birth certificate?'

'We don't deal with much paper. I can ask her.'

To Melanie's surprise he got out his phone and rang Queenie there and then. At least, she thought, at last he is taking this seriously. He walked around the office as he spoke. It wasn't a long conversation.

'No. She doesn't have anything. If I ever had one then it was lost in the fire. Everything was lost.'

'Well, I'm sure we can get a copy. I'll need your full name, date of birth, the hospital where you were born, parents' full names and so on.'

Robbie-Joe shrugged.

'I was two when I lost them. You know more about me than I do. I didn't even know I had another grandfather.'

'You should probably do this yourself,' Melanie said in a low voice, 'but I do have permission to support you through this.'

She tilted her computer screen for Robbie-Joe to see.

'We have to register with this website and then order a replacement birth certificate.'

Melanie typed in his name and that he lived at Stanlake Farm.

'When's your birthday?'

'What?'

'I need your birthday, obviously, in order to make sure we get the correct person. Are you sure you haven't got it at home? You would have needed it to get a passport.'

'I don't have a birth certificate. I don't have a passport and I don't have a birthday.'

Melanie stared at him. She wasn't sure if he was trying to be funny or just downright awkward and here she was trying her best to help him.

'Everyone has a birthday — the day you were born.'

'I remember Queenie telling me it was in the autumn because she said the day I was born she found the first ripe shiny conker and told me she'd always felt it was a lucky omen.'

'Can you be a bit more specific? September or October?'

His mobile phone rang. He nodded and left the office while he answered his call. Melanie hoped it was Queenie who'd found the all-important paperwork.

'I read a book once about a gypsy,' Anita said. 'He had loads of brothers and when asked when they were born they all said the first of January because it was after Christmas and around the time of the New Year. No-one knew exactly when.

'The mother had given birth at home with her mother-in-law and sister. They never went to a hospital and never registered the births. In their eyes there was no need. It was years ago and it wasn't a problem, but now . . . '

Melanie kept looking over at the door but while Anita had been talking she'd Googled whether birthdays were important in gypsy culture. It appeared not.

Robbie-Joe popped his head around the door.

'Got to go,' he said as he disappeared.

Melanie still had her mouth open when Anita came and sat by her desk.

'Try not to get too involved,' she warned. 'You do have other clients to attend to.'

'I do,' Melanie agreed as she slammed closed his file and put it to one side.

It was only while Melanie was eating her lunch and watching the cars go by that it dawned on her that Robbie-Joe drove a van and therefore must at some point have given his date of birth which would be on his driving licence.

However, she decided that she could

only do so much. Now it was up to him to contact her.

When Melanie visited her mother, as she always did a few times a week to help her out and cook her meals, she tried to ask about her past but could never quite bring herself to voice her thoughts.

She didn't want to hurt June Harper.

*   *   *

'Where have you been?' Melanie asked when Robbie-Joe next appeared in front of her over a week later. She checked herself, straightened up and asked if he had an appointment.

In response he waved a sheet of paper at her.

'You found it!'

'When I explained to Queenie why I needed it, she showed me an old tin chest that was my mother's. It was in there with some photos.'

'Excellent,' Melanie said, taking a photocopy of the birth certificate for evidence.

Suddenly she panicked, knowing that Mr Huntley had really been looking for a certificate of achievement, rather than this. She wondered if Mr Darcy would be pedantic. He could be and, on this occasion, she could understand why. Maybe Robbie-Joe's grandfather had been trying to ensure his grandson would better himself and get an education.

'I hope this will do the trick,' she said quietly as she handed him back the original. 'He's got someone with him at the moment, but bring that back in again and we'll see if he will accept it.'

Robbie-Joe looked as though he was going to say something, but then his phone rang again and he disappeared as before.

However, he returned the following evening just as they were packing up. His black wavy hair was wet and there was a vague smell of chlorine in the air. Melanie wondered if he used the local pool and its showers to bathe.

'Mr Darcy's in. He can see you now,'

Anita announced. She nodded at Melanie to finish the letter she was typing.

'Good, that's one down, eleven to go and still practically a whole year to go. Well done. Good start,' Mr Darcy was saying as Melanie entered the office. 'I am relieved it is a proper certificate. I didn't want you to bring in a marriage certificate, although I suppose I would have to accept it.'

Melanie's jaw dropped at the mention of a marriage certificate, but she managed to compose herself. Mr Darcy was still speaking.

'Let Melanie have it, so she can take a copy for evidence should anyone contest the will.'

Robbie-Joe handed over a green A4 card to Melanie. She looked down at the swimming certificate with that day's date, but waited because she, too, wanted to hear what his next challenge was.

Out of His Comfort Zone

Robbie-Joe kept pulling on the collar of his shirt. Melanie could tell he wasn't used to wearing a jacket, shirt and tie but she hoped no-one else would be any the wiser.

David Darcy's wife Eva, the sparrow, was an artist. She generally painted landscapes using watercolours. Tonight was the opening night at the gallery of her new exhibition. This evening was for art dealers and collectors. It was not open to the general public.

Anita and Melanie had been invited as special guests to the champagne reception in the Arts Centre. Melanie had persuaded Mr Darcy that it would be the ideal way for Robbie-Joe to achieve his next challenge. He had to visit somewhere new where he would be out of his comfort zone.

The Darcy brothers had discussed

the matter in private. Neither of them wanted a scene at the gallery but having spoken with Eva she was delighted to be able to help. She'd insisted her husband lend him a suit but as Robbie-Joe was several sizes bigger they sent him to a gentleman's outfitters who hired him one for the night.

'Stop staring at me,' Melanie whispered as they pretended to study a painting.

'But you're so beautiful,' Robbie-Joe said. 'I can't take my eyes off you.'

'Thank you, but you're here to look at the pictures. Quick, here comes Eva Darcy, she's the artist.'

'There's something I want to show you,' Eva said as she grabbed Robbie-Joe's arm and steered him deeper into the gallery.

Robbie-Joe glanced back at Melanie and in that instant she knew he was definitely out of his comfort zone, just as the challenge had required. Fortunately the Darcys witnessed his look of panic, too.

'He's scrubbed up well,' Peter admitted. 'You know, I wasn't sure about this.'

'Neither was I,' his brother admitted. 'But you know Eva, she was keen to help and we were all fond of Robert, so it's not as though he's just another client.'

'Robert?' Melanie repeated. 'Do you mean you knew Robert Huntley?'

Both men nodded.

'We were all at school together,' Peter said.

'Eva and I went to his wedding. I was amazed how young his bride looked,' David said.

'That's because she was only sixteen but they were very happy together, despite their differences.'

'She died in childbirth, didn't she?' Melanie asked.

She had been reading the file in the office.

'Yes, and that's when their daughter went to live with her mother's family. It broke Robert's heart but he knew it was the best thing for the child. There was no way he could have brought up a daughter on his own. He tried to keep in touch but he often worked abroad and I don't think the grandparents ever made him very welcome.'

'The only contact I remember him talking about,' Peter said, 'was when his daughter married. She was really young, too, and was marrying her cousin.

'He did go to their wedding. I recall him saying it was a grand affair with no expense spared. His only regret was that it wasn't him who gave her away but her grandfather.'

Eva returned soon after with Robbie-Joe by her side.

'I thought he'd prefer my floral pictures and he was able to name every single flower, even the wild ones. I was really impressed,' Eva said as though Robbie wasn't actually standing by her side.

She turned round to a waiter with a tray of champagne glasses and, like the perfect hostess, she handed round fresh drinks to everyone, including Robbie-Joe.

The plan was that Eva would assess

whether or not Robbie-Joe was out of his comfort zone and then sign a piece of paper to confirm that, and why.

The Darcy brothers felt this was the only way they could provide evidence for this particular task and Eva was an independent assessor.

Eva introduced Robbie-Joe to another artist and left them to discuss a painting. Melanie watched as beads of sweat appeared on his forehead. After a few minutes she could stand it no more and rescued him.

'Can we go now?' he asked. 'This is really not my sort of place, and this shirt is too tight.'

'You do look very handsome. I think you ought to dress up more often,' Melanie told him.

'I don't need a shirt and tie when I'm gardening.'

Eva gave Melanie a sympathetic nod and Melanie linked her arm through Robbie-Joe's.

'Come on,' she said. 'We can either get a taxi, or you can walk me to the station.'

'Have you eaten? I'm starving,' Robbie-Joe admitted.

At the thought of food, Melanie's stomach groaned. She'd been too busy getting ready to eat.

'I am a little hungry,' she confessed, 'but I really ought to go home. I've got a busy day tomorrow.'

Next door to the art gallery was an Italian restaurant.

'My treat, as a thank you,' Robbie-Joe said. 'But I'm still out of my comfort zone so I'll need your help.'

'No problem,' Melanie said cheerfully. 'We make a good team.'

Once again she linked arms with him and steered him into the restaurant. It was only later she told herself she'd acted that way due to the couple of glasses of champagne she'd had.

They were seated at a table for two in the corner. Melanie ordered spaghetti and Robbie-Joe did the same.

'Where did you get the swimming certificate from?' Melanie asked as she tried to make neutral conversation.

She was very aware of the way Robbie-Joe was studying her face.

'I do the café garden at the leisure centre and some children were coming out waving their certificates, so I asked how I could get one.'

'Are you telling me you just went into the pool and swum a few lengths and they gave you a certificate?'

'Actually, I've never been in the pool before, so I had to learn to swim. I haven't done much work these last couple of days, I've been having private lessons. But the coach was good and she told me I'd earned my certificate.'

'Wow, I'm impressed. I'd have given up as soon as Queenie found your birth certificate.'

'Well,' Robbie-Joe said. 'Maybe that's the difference between you and me. I never give up and you give up far too easily.'

The waiter arrived with their meals. Melanie ate in silence. Robbie-Joe had struck a chord.

Hadn't Anita accused her of giving

66

up so soon when she was fed up with her job and then couldn't find RJ Davies straightaway?

She looked again at Robbie-Joe in his smart hired suit and realised there was a lot more to this man than she had ever thought.

The Next Task

Task number three was to try something new. Robbie-Joe told Mr Darcy that he'd recently learned to swim, which had been a totally new experience for him, that he'd gone to the art gallery, another new venture and he'd taken Melanie for an Italian meal.

At this point Mr Darcy raised his eyebrows.

'I have a suggestion,' Melanie said. 'You'll appreciate that Mr Darcy and I don't know what is new to you and yet we have to prove that you can't have done it before or been there before. So we need to look for somewhere that has only just opened.'

'That does seem logical, Miss Harper,' Mr Darcy agreed.

'I've got it!' She laughed. 'I've just been reading in the paper about a new kind of entertainment called an Escape Room.

You are locked in a room and have an hour to solve various clues or puzzles in order to be released. We could do that!'

'We?'

'It's best done as a team because everyone has something to offer. I dare say we'll get a certificate if we're successful and that, along with the newspaper cutting that it's only just opened, can be our evidence.'

'You seem to have it all sewn up,' Mr Darcy said as he closed the file and handed it back to her.

Outside his office door Robbie-Joe stopped and shook his head.

'I don't like the idea of being locked in a room. I think it goes back to that fire when I had to be rescued.'

'They don't really lock us in, but they do close the door so we can concentrate. It'll be fun, trust me.'

Melanie headed straight for her desk and picked up the newspaper to show Robbie-Joe the picture. Straightaway she rang them.

'They say it's meant to be a

team-building exercise, so it's best in a group of about six.'

'I'll come,' Eva said, who had been waiting for her husband and had been chatting with Anita. 'You'll come, too, won't you, Anita?'

'I'm not sure . . . '

'It'll be fun, and we'll get David and Peter to make up the six,' Eva said decisively. 'That's settled, then. Melanie, you book it and I'll sort out the men. Are we all free on Saturday night?'

Melanie and Anita were the first to arrive at the Escape Room venue with Robbie-Joe shortly behind. David, Eva and Peter arrived soon after.

'Welcome to the Captain's Cabin,' the Escape Room manager said. 'You have one hour to solve the clues, unlock the padlock and free the ship's wheel which will save the ship and get it back on course. Don't worry, if you get really stuck I can offer you a small clue, but you'll still have to work to solve the problem. I'm not doing it for you. Good luck.'

With that he ushered them all into a medium-sized room and closed the door.

At first there didn't seem to be a lot in there. A chest sat in the centre. There was a padlocked ship's wheel under the window and a bookcase in the corner, but no obvious clues.

They searched the room. Above the wheel were two portraits with dates beneath them.

'I wonder if these dates are really the combination numbers for the padlock?' Melanie suggested. Systematically she tried each date, forward and backwards but it didn't seem to be the answer. Melanie tried each one again while the others searched the room.

Robbie-Joe found a loose floorboard and inside was a map. The co-ordinates led them to another clue which led them to a key. The key opened the chest and so on.

Later, Eva discovered one of the books on the shelf had been hollowed out and inside was yet another clue.

That moved them further on but they still had to find the correct combination for the ship's padlock. It was a simple idea but more difficult than it first seemed.

Melanie watched, fascinated by how everyone made different suggestions. She could see why a team had been a good idea.

To her surprise she'd found Robbie-Joe had a quick mind which was open to new ideas. He was obviously just as intelligent as the rest of them despite having received very little formal education. Melanie felt embarrassed for ever having doubted him and promised herself she wouldn't be so quick to judge in future.

Just as the 60-minute deadline was approaching, Robbie-Joe found a four-digit number, tried the padlock on the wheel and it worked. The lock opened and the chain holding the wheel fell to the ground. They had saved the ship with about a minute to go. Everyone cheered. They were each presented with a certificate and had photographs taken.

'It's all evidence,' Peter Darcy said as he smiled for the camera.

Melanie was beginning to look at her work colleagues in a different light. But she wasn't surprised when they decided it was late enough, they'd had enough excitement for one night and they were going home. It was barely eight o'clock.

'I can't be out too late,' Melanie said, conscious that only she and Robbie-Joe were left. 'I'm taking my mother out for the day tomorrow. She's been stuck inside all week and she's got a hospital appointment on Monday which she isn't looking forward to. I can't do anything about the outcome, but at least I can help take her mind off her appointment for a few hours.'

'Have you spoken to her yet?' Robbie-Joe asked. 'About your real parents.'

'No, not yet,' Melanie said. 'But I will.'

They walked along the high street

and into a nearby pub. Once settled into a corner Melanie stared down into her glass of wine.

'You're very quiet,' Robbie-Joe said after a while.

Melanie looked up and into his dazzling blue eyes.

'You remember when you had to produce a certificate?' she began.

Robbie-Joe nodded.

'Mr Darcy said he was glad you hadn't produced a marriage certificate and, well, it made me wonder, are you married?'

'No. Queenie had found me a girl and I was happy with her choice but what no-one knew was that this girl, Tara, loved a boy she'd met at school. On the eve of the wedding she ran off with this man.'

'Oh.'

'The worst thing was her mother, Nancy — she blamed me for it and everyone said I was cursed. I think she thought I must have upset Tara in some way.

'Queenie has tried to find me another girl but no-one wants someone with a curse around their neck.'

Melanie was about to say how stupid it all sounded, but stopped herself. There were several things she believed in that could be classed as silly, like ghosts or magic.

'And you?'

'Me?'

'Yes. You're called Miss Harper and you don't wear a ring and you're here with me now, so I know you're not married. But you must have had boy-friends.'

'I did have a couple of boyfriends at university but they weren't very serious. It was just good to have company to go out with to parties.'

'And now?'

'To be honest, I worked hard at uni-versity to get my degree. I was always aware that my parents had helped me get a place, and I didn't want to let them down.

'Now I've got a job, I spend most

evenings calling in on my mum. Her knees are bad and she finds it uncomfortable to stand for any length of time, but hopefully she'll soon have an operation that will put all that right.'

'Why don't you live with her?'

'She and Dad moved to an apartment in a retirement home several years ago. Dad was quite a bit older than Mum. They'd only been there a few months when he died. I was glad she had lots of friends around her.

'Everyone was very good but the rules of the home are that I can visit and sleep over in the guest room but I can't live there.'

'So you live alone?'

'No,' Melanie replied, not sure how much information she felt she ought to give him. 'I rent a room and the landlady is like a mother to me.'

'So we are alike,' Robbie-Joe said with his head on one side. 'Queenie brought me up and is like a mother to me. But neither of us knew our real mothers.'

A Day Out

Melanie had done her research for taking her mother out for the day. She picked June up after church on Sunday morning.

'What do you fancy?' Melanie asked, holding out a fistful of leaflets. 'The weather's OK, so we could visit a garden. This one is very small, so not much walking — or we could just go for a drive or an afternoon tea?'

'The garden sounds lovely,' June said. 'That's the one thing I miss. The retirement home is great, but the grounds are all for car parking. There are fields in the distance but we don't have any gardens.'

The garden was jam-packed with spring bulbs. Some of the trees had blossom and the sun shone for most of the time.

Although June always sounded bright

and cheerful, Melanie knew her well enough to realise it was all a show.

'Is it very painful?' she asked.

'Only when I walk,' June said. 'But it is so lovely to get out and about. Who knows, the hospital might have a cancellation and I'll be able to have my knee operation sooner rather than later.'

'Is that likely?'

'Well, stranger things have happened.'

Melanie leaned forward and kissed her mother.

'You're always so optimistic. Don't ever change.'

'Don't get soppy with me, you'll make me cry. How about a cup of tea and piece of cake?' June suggested in her matter-of-fact way.

Over a large pot of tea and generous slices of Victoria sponge they chatted about a range of topics.

Each time she spoke, Melanie knew she should ask about her real mother but again, didn't want to upset June who'd done so much for her.

Finally they made their way home.

It was only as she was heading for the door, that Melanie stopped and turned to her mother.

'I meant to say, I need to renew my passport,' she said, which was true. 'And I think I need my birth certificate,' she added, which may or may not have been true.

'That's not a problem,' June said. 'I don't know why I've still got it, anyway. You ought to keep hold of it yourself now you're grown up.'

June disappeared into her bedroom and Melanie let out a sigh of relief. She'd taken the first step in finding out more about her birth parents.

A few minutes later, June returned with a large envelope tied with a lilac ribbon.

'These are all bits and pieces for you. I've been meaning to give them to you but, well,' June hesitated, 'there's your adoption certificate and a few photos. I didn't want to upset you.'

'Upset me?'

'Well, it's not an easy subject to talk

about, especially when we're all so settled in our lives.'

Melanie gave June a huge hug.

'I'd never want to upset you, but just recently I have begun to wonder about my other parents. Why was I adopted?'

June gestured to a chair and Melanie sank down into it. She wondered why they'd never had this conversation before, but realised both had been avoiding it.

'We were told that although your parents loved you and they were happily married, they couldn't cope. I don't know, really, what this meant. I've often wondered if there was some illness in the family, or perhaps there were many children and perhaps they didn't have the resources to have another mouth to feed?'

'At least I know I was loved: doubly blessed, having two lots of parents care for me.' Melanie rose to make a move home.

'It can't have been easy for her,' June said. 'I mean, no woman ever gives up a child unless she has no other choice.'

'No, I suppose not. She must have had her reasons. Goodnight. I'll pop round in the week. Thanks again for a lovely day.'

Melanie made her way to her car with lots to think about.

She wondered whether June had told her what she wanted to hear, or whether it was true and she had been loved and wanted, but for some reason her parents couldn't keep her.

Perhaps she would never know.

★　★　★

When Melanie got in, Anita was curled up with her book — one she had borrowed from Peter Darcy's extensive collection of crime novels. Melanie tiptoed to her room and switched on her laptop.

She spent the next hour trying to find out what she could about her parents.

Her birth certificate showed her real name as being Mary, which had been changed on adoption to Melanie. Her father was called O'Mally but Melanie could only ever remember being called Harper after Brian Harper, her adoptive father.

To her surprise she discovered she'd been born in south-west Ireland in a small village called Ruan. She Googled her father's name. To her surprise and sorrow, up came a tribute to him — if, in fact, it was her father and not just someone with the same name.

She tried again with her mother's name but there were various people by the same name. It was impossible to tell which one, if any, were related to her.

★ ★ ★

Robbie-Joe called into the office on Monday morning. It was now mid-April and everyone was getting used to the frequent April showers.

'I've come for the next one,' Robbie-Joe said with a big grin. 'You were right, the challenges weren't as bad as I thought.'

'I wouldn't speak too soon,' Melanie

warned. 'The next task might be really difficult.'

'I didn't say it was easy to learn to swim and I didn't like having to dress up for that art gallery, but the Escape Room was fun and you didn't give up. Perhaps I misjudged you.'

Melanie looked around but Anita was in with Mr Darcy and no-one else was around.

'I plucked up the courage to speak with my adoptive mother. I know a bit more about my other parents. I was originally born Mary O'Mally from Ruan in Ireland.'

'And are you going to meet them?' Robbie-Joe asked.

'I'm not even sure if they're alive,' Melanie admitted. 'It's been quite a lot to take in. I think I'll just take it one step at a time. I can't relate to being Mary O'Mally. It seems as though she's someone totally different.'

Robbie-Joe paced up and down as he waited for Mr Darcy to be free. The building was old with low beams and every so often Robbie-Joe had to duck to avoid knocking into the wooden beams.

'Is something wrong?' Melanie asked. 'You seem anxious.'

'I have an appointment,' he told her. 'I'm meeting someone at twelve.'

'Oh,' Melanie said, feeling disappointed. 'I'm sure Mr Darcy won't keep you much longer.'

In due course Robbie-Joe was summoned into Mr Darcy's office. The next task, challenge number four, was that he had to improve a skill.

'I gather you run your own gardening business,' Mr Darcy said. 'Is there an area that you feel could be improved? Perhaps there is a gardening course you could enrol on?'

'Business is going well. I like to keep it simple. I go to the same people all the time and just help them keep their gardens neat and tidy. I don't do any fancy landscaping or anything complicated. I just mow the lawns, weed the beds and do a few jobs for the old folks.'

'Well, that seems like a good business

plan,' Mr Darcy agreed, 'but haven't you ever thought about learning a new skill?'

Robbie-Joe looked down into his lap. Melanie watched him and thought he looked uncomfortable rather than searching for inspiration.

'My handwriting's not good,' he said at last.

'Perhaps you can write something out for Miss Harper and then see what you can do to improve upon it, say within the next month. I wouldn't advise you to leave it much longer.'

Robbie-Joe nodded and followed Melanie out of Mr Darcy's office. She went straight to her desk, picked up a blank sheet of paper and a pen and offered them to him.

'Write something down, or copy a paragraph from the newspaper, so we've got a before and after to keep as evidence.'

'Why do you always need evidence? Who would you show it to?' he asked.

'It will probably sit, collecting dust,

in some file, but you never know who might come in and ask to see if we have done our job properly, and made sure you achieved all the twelve goals before Mr Darcy feels he is able to release the funds that your grandfather left for you.'

Robbie-Joe sat at the desk and wrote laboriously. Once again he looked out of his comfort zone. Writing was definitely not something he did very often, Melanie thought.

After a while he handed the paper to Melanie who signed and dated it and popped it in the file.

'Must be off,' he said and without a backward glance he was gone.

Melanie looked again at the sheet. He'd painstakingly written out the alphabet in a scrawl that looked more like the writing of a doctor than a gardener.

The Search Continues

That evening Melanie popped in on her mother and made her tea. She did a little cleaning for her and together they did a crossword, then she made her way home to her lodgings with Anita McCree.

Once again Anita was avidly reading another of Mr Darcy's crime novels which he had lent her.

'This one's really good. I've only got half a dozen pages to go and the murderer could be any one of three suspects. It's really tense.'

'I'll leave you to it,' Melanie said as she made herself a hot drink and disappeared up to her room.

She spent the next hour on Facebook searching for the Bridget O'Mally that was her mother. There was only one who lived in Ruan but she looked too young, but then maybe the photograph had been taken a while ago.

Melanie sent her a carefully-worded message, to see if she was likely to be the right person.

After that, Melanie soaked in a lovely hot bath, hoping that it would help her sleep soundly. It seemed to have the opposite effect and once again she was wide awake during the early hours of the morning.

This time it was Robbie-Joe who was keeping her awake. She had been dreaming of his sparkling blue eyes and his dazzling smile. She told herself again and again that business and pleasure do not mix. He was a client and she should not get involved. She knew that they had little in common and yet there was something that kept drawing her back to Robbie-Joe.

Until earlier that day, she had thought he'd felt that same feeling. She was sure he'd felt an attraction between them, but today he'd mentioned that he was meeting someone else.

Of course, it could be someone

needing their garden tidied or lawn cut, but it had been the way he'd said it. There was something secretive about it, yet there was absolutely no reason why he should keep Melanie informed of any new girlfriend, if that was whom he was meeting.

As Melanie tossed and turned she told herself the best way to deal with the situation was to keep professional at work and, above all, to keep herself busy. She would stop every time she thought of Robbie-Joe and force herself to think of something or someone else. But that was easier said than done.

The following morning passed by fairly quickly but the afternoon dragged. Robbie-Joe's image kept popping into her mind and she couldn't concentrate on the report she was meant to be reading.

'Do you want a cuppa?' she asked Anita.

'It's a bit early for a tea break.'

'I know, but I can't focus at the moment and I thought maybe a cup of tea would help.' Melanie could tell that Anita did not approve. 'Oh, no, we've got no milk. I'll nip next door and fetch some.'

Without waiting for Anita to respond, Melanie picked up her jacket and left the office.

The queue in the supermarket was long. Melanie looked at the people around her and wondered what they would do if they were set a series of tasks which they had to achieve before they could be rewarded at the end. How well would she have done, if she'd been in that situation?

It would not have been a problem finding a certificate — she had been well educated and had a whole file full of certificates she was proud of. However, she knew she didn't like to be out of her comfort zone and had to admit that, whenever she'd visited Queenie at the trailer site, she was very much out of place and uncomfortable.

As for something new, she, too, had enjoyed their team-building experience and had particularly liked seeing both Mr David and Mr Peter in a different light. It had not made any obvious lasting impression on the way the office was run. They had reverted to their serious expressions whenever they were in the office.

Melanie paid for the milk and wondered what skill she would most like to improve. At school she had tried to learn another language but knew it wasn't her strong point. Perhaps she ought to go to evening classes to develop her language skills and meet some new people?

When she returned to the office Anita had been called in to work with Mr David and Mr Peter had gone out to see a client. She made herself a cup of tea and sat back down at her desk.

It wasn't any easier to read the report she'd been trying to get through. She was distracted by the file of Robbie-Joe's which now sat on her desk waiting to be filed until he came in again.

Melanie reached for the large buff folder and flicked through the papers. She was intrigued to know what the next task would be, but all she found was a pile of sealed envelopes, each one numbered. She wondered if Mr Darcy knew what each one contained. Someone must know what secrets the envelopes held.

Her thoughts were interrupted by the phone. She had to calm an anxious buyer who was worried about the sale of his current home because he thought his sale was about to fall through. The rest of the afternoon flew by as Melanie worked through her conveyancing file.

★　★　★

The weeks went by and the days grew warmer. The spring bulbs died down, giving way to summer flowers and longer days. It was nearly a month since Melanie had seen Robbie-Joe. She'd thought about him but had no cause to contact him until today, when Mr Darcy had asked her to get in touch with him and to see how he was getting on improving his skills.

Melanie called him.

'Hi, it's me, Melanie. Mr Darcy was

wondering how you were getting on with your current task?'

'I'll call in,' he told her and the line went dead.

Later that afternoon Robbie-Joe appeared. His large frame still filled the doorway but there was something different about him. Melanie watched as he hung up his jacket and approached her desk.

She looked at his hair, which had been cut, but that wasn't what it was that was different about him.

He held out a small exercise book. It looked like one that Melanie had used at school. The pages were specifically designed for improving handwriting.

'Open it,' he instructed.

Melanie flicked through the pages. The first few were covered with a spidery scrawl just like the sheet he had produced for her, which still sat in his file. The latter pages showed carefully formed letters and words repeated again and again. He was obviously proud of his efforts.

She handed him a blank sheet of

paper and a pen and asked him to write out the alphabet as he'd done a month or so ago.

'Haven't you got any lined paper?' he asked.

'I have, but that won't be a true comparison,' she told him. 'It's got to be the same to show a proper improvement, Robbie-Joe.'

'Joe,' he told her. 'I like to be called Joe now.'

'Oh,' Melanie said, wondering what else had changed about him. 'I'll try to remember that.'

He sat and leaned on the corner of her desk as he had done before, but this time he quickly finished the task. Melanie had been watching him. He seemed so much more confident on this occasion.

His handwriting had certainly improved but it couldn't just be that. Perhaps he was happier in the summer. His job must be a lot easier in the better weather and with the longer days, she thought.

Once again Melanie signed and dated the sheet and as soon as Mr Darcy was free they went into his office and produced the exercise book and two sheets to show how much his handwriting had improved.

Unusually, Mr Darcy was in a chatty mood. For the first time he spoke to Joe about Robert Huntley, his grandfather.

Melanie sat back and watched as Joe asked questions about the relation he'd never known. She noticed how he sat back in his chair and laid his hands in his lap. On other occasions he'd been fidgety and had appeared anxious. He really did seem much more confident in himself today and she wondered what had happened in his life to bring about this change.

At the end of the meeting Mr Darcy stood, as he always did, to signal that time was up. Joe thanked Mr Darcy and offered him his hand. His handshake seemed strong and confident. Perhaps business had been going well?

Mr Darcy had been satisfied that the challenge had been met and had opened the envelope marked number five. Robbie-Joe, or Joe as he now liked to be known, had to take part in some charity work. Joe had just nodded to show he'd understood, shaken hands with Mr Darcy and left.

'There's something different about him,' Melanie said aloud to Anita once they watched him cross the street to the little café opposite.

'He walks taller,' Anita said. 'Do you think it's the tasks that are doing him some good?'

'Would they really make a difference?' Melanie asked.

'Who knows? But I think I would feel good about myself if each month I felt I was achieving something over and above my daily routine. Perhaps we should all try to take part. What was his challenge this time?'

'He has to do some charity work,' Melanie told her.

'Shall we do something, too?'

'Any ideas?' Melanie asked but Anita shook her head and said she'd have to think about it.

They didn't have to think for very long because a few days later Joe returned with a poster asking if they would display it in their window.

'I'm helping at the school fair. They are a registered charity. My cousin's got some donkeys and we're going to run a stall giving donkey rides to the kids and taking their photos. It's a fund-raising event for the school. They need to buy new playground equipment.'

'Well, that seems like a good cause,' Anita said, taking the poster from him. 'I will check with Mr Darcy, but I can't see why we wouldn't be able to display it for you. In fact, Melanie and I were talking about supporting some charity work, so perhaps we'll come along and see the donkeys.'

'You'd be most welcome,' Joe said, giving a little bow. 'Some of my nieces and nephews go to the school and two of my cousins are running the cake stall. You should try Alice's cakes, they're the best.'

That evening when Melanie called round to see her mother, she asked if she'd be interested in going to the school fair at the weekend.

'I'd like to get out,' June said. 'The forecast is good but I'll have to see how the knee is.'

'Well, we don't need to make up our minds until the morning, so I'll call round on Saturday and see how you feel. Anita said she'd like to come. I think she's always had a soft spot for donkeys. Apparently she used to help out at a donkey sanctuary and she wants to make sure these ones are well looked after.'

Melanie was tired by the time she got back to her room. She quickly switched on her laptop to check her e-mails before she got ready for bed.

To her surprise, after months of silence there was a message from a Bridget O'Mally who had once lived in Ruan, Ireland, and said she had information that Melanie might be interested in.

Melanie stared at the computer screen. Was this her real mother making contact with her? Would they ever meet, and if they did what on earth would they say to each other after 27 years?

She couldn't decide how to respond. She decided to sleep on it and answer the following day when she was more alert. The last thing she wanted to do was to upset her other mother.

Donkey Derby

Joe was so busy helping children get on to a donkey's back safely that it was a while before he noticed Melanie watching him.

'I didn't realise you'd have so many,' she exclaimed as she and Anita approached a pen full of donkeys. 'Is it all right to stroke them?'

'Boxer is fine, but Cassidy is a bit grumpy today. I think he's hot.'

Anita stroked Boxer and chatted away to him as though he were her personal pet.

'I'm impressed,' she said. 'I feared they might not be in the best of health but all these animals looked very well cared for.'

'My cousin thinks the world of his donkeys. I sometimes think he prefers them to people.' Joe laughed. 'He's supposed to be coming over to give me a break in a minute. Shall we go for a walk round when he comes?'

'I mustn't be too long,' Melanie said, 'I've left Mum in the tea tent.'

'I'd offer to bring a donkey over to see her, but I don't think I'd trust one near the cakes — they can steal food quick as any goat.'

It was some time before Joe was relieved by his cousin. Anita and Melanie had made their way to June in the tea tent.

'Ladies,' Joe said, 'what can I get you? More tea and cake? I'm told the carrot cake is delicious, but then so are the scones.'

'I'll give you a hand,' Anita offered, leaving Melanie with her mother.

'What a charming young man,' June said. 'Do you know him?'

'His name's Joe Davies, he comes into the office quite often. I thought I was getting to know him, but now I'm not so sure. He's changed a lot recently and I don't seem to be able to reach him.'

'Well, there's only one person who can put that right,' June told her. 'I wouldn't hang about if I were you.'

Melanie blushed as Joe returned to the table with a tray of tea and cakes.

June asked Joe about himself and discovered he was a gardener.

'I wish you'd come and make us a garden at the retirement home where I live,' she said.

'I don't think there's any room for a garden, Mum,' Melanie said. 'All the spare ground's been used for car-parking space.'

'It's such a shame. I do miss my garden. We haven't even got anywhere to sit out and enjoy the sunshine. No-one wants to watch cars coming and going all day long.'

'Will you be coming into the office again next week?' Melanie asked Joe. 'I expect you'll want to know what's in your next envelope?'

'I'll try to get in but Queenie's not been well and I've been really busy. It's always the same in the summer:

everyone wants their garden to look colourful, neat and tidy.'

Melanie wanted to tell him her news about making contact with her other mother but got the distinct impression that she was being kept at arm's length.

'I'm sorry to hear about Queenie,' she said. 'Please send her my regards.'

Joe finished his cake and made his excuses.

'I ought to get back to the donkeys, but good to see you all and thank you for supporting the school.'

He waved as he disappeared and was swallowed up by the crowd.

'A very nice young man,' June said again. 'He wasn't wearing a wedding ring, I noticed.'

'Shall we go and see the crafts?' Melanie suggested, changing the subject.

'Don't worry, I'll clear the table,' Anita said. 'I'll catch you up in a bit. I think I saw Mr Peter in the queue.'

Melanie and June wandered around the homemade crafts making a few purchases.

'Anita's taking her time,' Melanie said when they came to the end of the field. Just then they saw an ambulance slowly make its way across the school field toward the tea tent.

'Oh, dear, I hope no-one's been seriously hurt,' June said. 'Or it's not a child falling off a donkey. That could be nasty.'

'Just stay here, Mum, while I go and check.'

Melanie found a group clustered around Anita McCree, who was holding her arm.

'I tripped and fell,' she explained. 'The paramedic thinks I've broken my arm. I can't move it and it does hurt.'

'Do you want me to come with you to hospital?' Melanie asked.

'No, I'll be fine. Peter's taking me. You go back to your mother and we'll catch up later.'

When Melanie returned to the craft area her mother was nowhere to be found.

'Have you seen a woman with a

walking stick?' she asked. 'She's wearing a blue skirt.'

No-one had seen her. Melanie wandered round the stalls searching for her mother, thinking that she might have to resort to the tent labelled 'Lost children' and ask them to put out a message on the loudspeaker for her mum.

'There you are,' Melanie said at last when she recognised the blue skirt and found her mum petting the donkeys.

'Aren't they friendly?' June said. 'Did you find Anita?'

'She's had a fall and possibly broken her arm. The paramedics suggested she went to the hospital for an x-ray.'

'Does she need help?' Joe asked.

'I did offer, but she said she'd be fine. Peter Darcy was with her. I imagine she'll have quite a wait at the hospital. I'll call her later.'

It was getting late before Melanie got home. She was surprised to find Anita and Joe sitting in the lounge, laughing together.

'Joe's my hero,' Anita said. 'He came

to collect me from the hospital. Peter had kindly taken me and stayed for a few hours but he'd promised to help Eva with her next exhibition.'

'That was very kind of you, Joe,' Melanie said with a smile.

'Well, I ought to be going now. Goodnight.'

'There's no need to go on my account,' Melanie said quickly, but Joe was already standing up and clearing away their mugs.

Rising to the Occasion

'Well done, Joe,' Mr Darcy said as he re-read the letter Joe had given him. 'That's an impressive amount of money to fund-raise by giving donkey rides. The charity must be very pleased.'

'I didn't do it on my own. They're my cousin's animals. I was just there to help on the day.'

Mr Darcy looked again at the letter.

'Can we keep this thank-you letter as evidence of your charity work?'

'Of course. I don't need it. What's next on the list?' Joe asked.

Mr Darcy opened the next envelope with the flourish of a magician.

'It says you are to make a personal sacrifice. You'll probably want to give that some thought and get back to me as usual.'

Mr Darcy rose to shake Joe's hand.

'Actually, I'd like a word with you, in

private,' Joe said, looking in Melanie's direction.

'Oh, yes, of course,' she said and made a quick exit.

About half an hour later Joe emerged from the office, nodded to Melanie and left. Melanie felt a pang of disappointment but, with Anita being off work with her broken arm, she had more to do than to worry about what Joe had said to Mr Darcy.

★ ★ ★

'Miss Harper,' David Darcy said on Monday morning, 'do you know anything about the Simmons' case?'

Melanie reached for a pile of similar-looking brown files and pulled one out.

'It's all here, Mr Darcy. I've put a Post-it note on the top to tell you what's outstanding.'

'Excellent work, Miss Harper, well done,' he said.

It was praise, although Melanie detected an element of surprise that she even knew which case he had been talking about.

Melanie prided herself on being organised and efficient. As soon as Anita had to make the decision not to come into work, she'd gone into the office and made a list of all the current cases, then located the files and systematically gone through them, making a note of what stage they were at and what needed to be done next.

The exercise had taken her the best part of the day and her daily correspondence had fallen behind, but she realised it had been worth it in the end because it had saved her time and the following day she'd worked hard to catch up on all the outstanding correspondence.

During the time Anita was convalescing, Melanie had extended her hours, going in earlier and not finishing until much later. She found she was much happier in her work because she felt she was just about keeping on top of everything, and also because she was in charge.

She liked being given the chance to really get her teeth into the job, rather than always feeling like someone's assistant or the office junior. She was delighted that both Mr Peter and Mr David seemed pleased, and relieved that she'd just got on with the job.

However, after the first week she did speak with Mr Peter and suggested they employ a temp.

'I need someone who can just do the basic things like filing, providing hot drinks for clients and making the occasional phone call to chase something up.'

'Of course, if that's what it takes to keep the office running smoothly. I must say I have been impressed by what I've seen this week. We have always depended so much on Anita. I didn't think we'd manage at all without her.'

'She trained me well,' Melanie told him. 'But I must admit, I've really enjoyed feeling that I'm more involved with what's going on.'

'Is the temp something you can

organise?' he asked.

'I'll make enquiries,' Melanie said. 'I'll double-check the costs with you before I finally commit us.'

'Good thinking,' he said and then, almost as an afterthought, he called her back into the office. 'We have decided, under the circumstances, that you deserve a pay rise. We'll obviously pay you for your additional hours and a bonus while you are covering for Miss McCree.

'When she returns and you revert to your previous role, you will be on a higher annual income and, should a suitable course become available and Miss McCree is back, then we would consider offering you that further training.'

Melanie looked at Mr Darcy in surprise. He generally held the purse strings very close to his heart. That made her feel all the more valued by his generous offer.

'Thank you,' she said, taking the handwritten piece of paper with his calculations with her. She felt good that she wasn't being taken for granted.

Melanie had never appreciated the long summer evenings as much as she did this year. After a full day's work, although tired, she was still able to do a few chores for her mother at the end of the day.

'And how is Anita?' June asked. 'Is she still in pain?'

'I think she's more comfortable now, but she's frustrated because it's so restricting having one arm out of action.'

Melanie was all too aware that she should return soon to her lodgings and check on her landlady to see if there was anything she needed help with.

The one blessing, Melanie thought, was that as soon as her head hit the pillow she would be asleep. Gone were the sleepless nights. She found it easier to put Robbie-Joe — or Joe as he now wished to be called — out of her mind. Well, almost. Her mind was fully occupied with work and with caring for the women around her.

It was late by the time Melanie arrived home but the light was still on in the lounge. As usual, Anita was there reading yet another of Peter's crime novels.

'Can I get you anything?' Melanie asked.

'I've had visitors tonight and they've been very good, and made sure we've all had tea. They even washed up. Come and sit down with me a minute.'

Melanie joined her in the other fireside chair.

'Is everything all right?' she asked. A moment of panic shot through her but Anita was smiling.

'I'm as well as can be expected but I will be so pleased when I can have this plaster removed.'

'It's only another week or so, isn't it?'

'Actually, it's fifteen days, not that I'm counting,' Anita admitted. 'Now, the reason I wanted to speak to you was that your mother just called.'

113

Melanie was surprised. She'd only just left her. Then she thought perhaps Anita had been referring to her birth mother, Bridget, but Melanie was sure she hadn't given her the number.

'June was saying she'd seen an advert for a very comfortable-looking hotel by the sea. She'd like a change of scenery and would have invited you, but obviously you're very busy at the moment. So she's asked me.'

As much as Melanie would have loved to spend a week by the sea with her mum, now was not the right time and it would help her considerably if neither June nor Anita needed her assistance for a while.

'That sounds like an excellent idea,' she agreed. 'When do you go?'

'We'll go on Saturday morning, if you could take us to the station?'

'That'll be fine and I can pick you up the following week.'

★　★　★

Over the next few days, Melanie was able to help both women pack. They were both excited about their trip away.

'I think it will do us the world of good to have a change of scenery and I do enjoy Anita's company. I think she's fed up of being at home now,' June said.

'She's read all Mr Darcy's collection of crime novels. I've had to get some more for her from the library,' Melanie said.

'I hope she's not going to have her head in a book all week,' June said with a smile. 'I asked her along because I wanted someone to talk to and to take a stroll in the garden with.'

'We've only packed one book,' Melanie told her. 'She's looking forward to breathing in some sea air.'

Melanie smiled. Both June and Anita's enthusiasm reminded her of the excitement she felt when she'd been away on a school trip with her best friend.

On Saturday morning she dropped

June and Anita off at the station and was able to help them both with their luggage.

'I'm sure there will be somebody at the other end who will be able to help you get the cases off, and find you a trolley.'

As soon as she'd waved them off, Melanie headed back to the car and decided that while she was out and about she ought to go and call on Queenie who had had a summer cold that had gone to her chest.

She parked along the street and walked the last part of the way to the trailer site. The first thing she noticed was the huge mountain of black rubbish bags waiting to be collected.

She sighed and thought how foolish she had been to assume that one phone call had sorted the problem for good. She took a few photos with her phone in order to shame the council into collecting the refuse.

It dawned on Melanie that she wasn't sure whether Joe actually lived in the same caravan as his grandmother, or whether he now had one of his own. She was disappointed not to see his white van parked in the bays near the entrance, but then she guessed he would be very busy with his gardening business at this time of year.

She walked up to Queenie's home and knocked on the door. A dog barked and she braced herself for a confrontation with the angry man who'd greeted her in the past. As she feared, he was the one who answered the door, but she could hear other voices, too.

'I've come to see Queenie, if she's up to visitors,' Melanie explained.

The man stepped aside to let her in. As usual, the van looked spotless. She wondered if Queenie had been confined to her bed.

A woman with long brown hair swept up into a ponytail and large earrings greeted her warily.

'May I see Queenie?' Melanie asked politely. 'My name's Melanie Harper. I have been before.'

There followed a short conversation between this younger woman and Queenie. It sounded as though they were speaking a foreign language.

The booming voice of Queenie called from within her bedroom that she should come in. Melanie remembered how surprised she'd been that the diminutive woman should have such a strong voice.

Again she was reminded of Queen Victoria and wondered if that was where she got her name.

Queenie was dressed from head to toe in black, just as before. Melanie briefly wondered if she was in mourning. She sat on the edge of her bed, her knitting in her hands. As Melanie entered, she gestured to a little wooden chair in the corner of the room.

'What's that you're making?' Melanie asked, striking up a conversation. There didn't seem to be a pattern nearby for Queenie to follow.

'Baby clothes,' she replied. 'There's always a need for new baby things.'

Melanie watched as Queenie knitted.

118

She felt she'd aged since they'd last met.

'Have you seen Robbie-Joe recently — sorry, I mean Joe?'

'I haven't heard much from him. I think he's working away or he's got some woman.' Queenie paused. 'He's changed ever since you came on the scene with your offers of money.'

'I haven't offered him anything. All I was doing was my job. His grandfather died and left him money, but it's more complicated than that,' Melanie said, knowing that it wasn't her business to say too much. 'I think he's changed, too. He seems more confident and . . . '

'Absolutely,' Queenie said, her sharp bird-like eyes looking up and meeting Melanie's. 'He stood up to my brother Frank. No-one's ever done that before.'

She chuckled to herself.

'Good to see. A man needs to be strong if he's to get on in the world. I always knew he was destined for big things.'

'Is Frank the man who's often here when I've visited before?' Melanie asked.

119

'He can come across as fierce, like his dog,' Queenie agreed, 'but he's only trying to protect me.'

'I understand. I often wished I had a big brother to protect me when I was at school.'

'Why are you here now?'

'When I last saw Joe, he said you weren't well. I brought you these,' Melanie said, handing over a pretty box of chocolates. 'Is there anything I can do for you?'

'I don't need your help,' Queenie said, accepting the gift. Her words were gruff but Melanie thought it was just her pride speaking. 'I suppose you want me to give him another message?'

'No. No message. I dare say he might call in to the office sometime. I'm sure he's a very busy man, especially during the summer months.'

'He's not with you, then?' Queenie asked. 'I thought you'd taken him away from me.'

Melanie wasn't sure how to respond. She hadn't seen or heard from him for a few weeks and she had no idea where he was living if it wasn't at the trailer site. It appeared that Queenie was as much in the dark about his whereabouts as she was. Melanie passed on her best wishes and said goodbye to Queenie.

As she left she reflected on Robert Huntley's will. Initially she'd felt he was a cunning man who had tried to help his grandson develop by leaving these tasks for him to undertake, but now she wondered if perhaps they were having an adverse effect on Joe.

For the first time in what felt like ages, Melanie had a bit of time to herself. She called in at the hair salon and asked for a new hair style. As much as she liked her long hair, she felt her new status in life demanded a modern, new look.

An hour later she walked out, delighted with the new style that was going to be so much easier to manage. Every so often she caught a glimpse of herself in a shop window and felt it was going to take a bit of getting used to.

Surprises All Round

On Monday morning Melanie was in the office early, preparing the work for the day ahead. She knew it was going to be a busy week as she had two property sales she'd been working on that were both due to come to completion by the end of the week.

The phone rang. Melanie was expecting Peter Darcy to call and update her on his early morning meeting.

'Melanie Harper?' an unfamiliar male voice said.

'Yes, good morning, how can I help you?'

'Actually, it's more of how I can help you,' he said. 'I work for a recruitment agency and I've been asked to contact you with regard to a new position.'

'When are you sending me this temp? I had expected her at nine this morning and she hasn't arrived.'

'I think there's been a misunderstanding. I don't work for a temporary staff agency. I work with career professionals helping them make executive moves. I'm offering you the chance of a new job. It'll pay double what you currently earn with numerous perks.'

'But I've got a job. I need a temp,' Melanie snapped, anxious to be able to get on with her work.

'At least let me send you the information. I promise you, it'll be something you ought to consider.'

'You can send it, but just at the moment I really need to get on. Thank you for your call.'

'Was that Peter?' David Darcy asked.

'No,' Melanie said. She could feel herself blushing.

'Is something wrong?'

'No, nothing at all. I'd been expecting the temp to arrive this morning and she hasn't turned up. Did you want to speak to Mr Peter when he calls?'

'Yes, put him through to me, thank you.'

No sooner had Mr David closed his office door, when a tall figure appeared, blocking the sunlight from coming through the doorway.

Melanie did a double take. It was a very smart-looking Joe Davies. How different he looked now from when she had first tracked him down. Then he had looked uncomfortable and nervous in the solicitors' building, but now he stood tall and proud.

'Good morning. I'm afraid Mr Peter isn't in at the moment. Do you want to make an appointment to come back and see him?'

Joe stood in the doorway, looking at her but not responding to her question.

'I'm sorry,' he said at last. 'What did you say?'

'He's not in. Do you want an appointment? Or will you just call in when it suits you?'

'I'll call back,' Joe replied and turned to go. 'I like your hair. It suits you.'

She patted her hair, pleased he'd noticed.

A few minutes later, he'd returned with a toolbox in his hand.

'I noticed his door didn't shut properly when I was last here. Would now be a good time to mend it, while he's out?'

'He didn't say anything about you doing any maintenance for him,' Melanie said, 'but it would make sense to do it now. You're not going to make too much noise, are you?'

Joe busied himself adjusting the hinges on the door and checking how it closed. The floorboards were uneven and so was the ceiling. The door swung to and fro, either jarring on one or the other, but eventually he got it just right so that it opened and closed perfectly.

Melanie had just put the kettle on so she made them both a drink. She had hoped for the opportunity to tell him of her visit to Queenie and that she'd made contact with her birth mother but the phone kept ringing and then Mr Darcy returned. He and Joe chatted in his office for a while and then Joe left while she was out of the office.

'Has he done the last task?' Melanie asked. 'I'll update the file.'

'We're still debating that.' Mr Darcy laughed. 'Don't worry. He'll be back,' he said cryptically.

★   ★   ★

That night Melanie woke in the early hours. Something had disturbed her. She lay still in bed and listened to the familiar sounds of the house.

Miss McCree was away on holiday, so she was alone. There didn't seem to be anything untoward, but she knew she had woken for a reason.

She pulled the covers up around her neck and tried to recall whether she'd had an unpleasant dream but she didn't think she'd been dreaming at all.

There was a strange glow coming from her window. She got up to pull the curtains together and in doing so noticed that somewhere in the distance there was a fire.

From what she could tell it looked serious. Even in the darkness she could see smoke and flames drifting up into the air. There seemed to be several blue lights flashing, and there were sirens wailing in the distance.

Melanie watched the scene for a while trying to work out where it was coming from, but it was too dark to see any landmarks. Eventually she climbed back into bed and fell asleep.

The following morning she was aware of the smell and even the taste of the smoke in the air. It wasn't until she got to work and nipped into the super-market nearby that she learned of the source of the fire.

'It was the gypsy camp,' one woman said. 'Totally destroyed, it was. My husband's a firefighter and they were there all night but they couldn't save anything.'

'Was anyone hurt?' Melanie asked.

Her first thought had been Joe, despite Queenie saying that she'd not seen him around lately.

'He didn't say, but it'll be on the news later,' the woman told her.

Melanie returned to the office and put on the local television news. There were pictures of the scene, the fire blazing all night and then the blackened carcasses of the mobile homes. It looked like some strange sci-fi land where all was black, and eerie wisps of smoke spiralled up into the early morning air.

It was only when, at last, the news reporter confirmed that although the residents were suffering from shock, there were no casualties, that Melanie realised she'd been holding her breath.

She reached for her phone and texted Joe. Queenie said he'd been living elsewhere and she wondered if he was even aware of what had happened. There was no reply.

Melanie wondered if he could read or understand her message. She dialled his number and left a voicemail.

★　★　★

Later that morning Melanie rang the hotel where June and Anita were staying. She wanted to reassure them that everything was all right just in case they saw anything on the news.

'What happened?' Anita asked.

'It's too early to tell, and I haven't been able to get hold of anyone yet, but the fire must have been pretty intense. Those mobile homes are made of metal and the fire spread really quickly.'

'And Joe?'

'Nothing,' Melanie said. 'I've left loads of messages but he hasn't been in touch. You know what he's like. I'll let you know as soon as I hear anything.'

'Please do that,' Anita said.

'They were saying on the local news that all the residents were being put up in a local village hall overnight and they had had an offer from a hotel to house them until the council could decide what was the best course of action.'

Melanie really wanted to shut up the office and make her way to the scene of the fire but knew that was out of the question.

The TV news reporters were interviewing several people. Everyone had their own theory of what had started the fire. Some said it was a cigarette, someone else suggested a faulty heater which was unlikely as it had been a warm night.

Melanie continued to watch. She couldn't bring herself to leave the screen just in case she saw someone she knew.

Her ears pricked up when two men talked about the bags of rubbish that had been allowed to accumulate near the entrance to the site.

The rubbish had been there for weeks. There had been getting on for a hundred black plastic bags of waste. It was common for these bags to heat up and sweat during the course of the long summer days.

Many of the residents had begun to complain about the smell. No-one had thought about the risk of a fire.

Melanie checked her phone, firstly to see if she'd missed a call from Joe but there was still no word from him.

Then she retrieved the photographs she'd taken of the piles of rubbish and went over to her desk, where she loaded the pictures on to the computer and sent them to the council.

Were they responsible for the fire?

Just then a young girl knocked on the door and announced that the agency had sent her.

'You needed an office junior?' she asked quietly.

'I do. Come on in and I'll show you around,' Melanie said, with one eye on the TV news.

Most of the information she'd heard several times before as they kept repeating what they already knew. She listened anyway, just in case there was any news of Joe.

Melanie showed the temp around and gave her some filing to get on with.

'We don't usually have the television on but one of our clients might have been in the area and I want to check that he, and his family, are safe.'

'It still smells awful out there,' the girl said. 'You can taste the smoke and my clothes smell dreadful. Even my eyes are sore and I haven't been that close to the fire. I'll have to wash my hair again tonight.'

'I know it's bad,' Melanie said sharply, 'but at least you have a home to go back to.'

'I suppose so,' the young girl said, who was only a teenager.

She bowed her head and got on with her job, only glancing up at the TV screen every so often.

'I'm sorry,' Melanie said a few minutes later. 'I shouldn't have bitten your head off then. It's just that I know people who live there and I'm worried.'

'You should try the other channel. Their reports are much better.'

'I thought they would just show the same pictures,' Melanie said, reaching for the remote and changing channels.

She stood back and stared at the

television. It was like watching a movie. The fire was blazing, the blue lights flashing, people being brought out on stretchers and taken away in ambulances.

There were emotional reunions and in the centre of it all was a large man pointing out to the fireman where to go.

The smoke was obviously hampering their vision but these brave men didn't give up until everyone was accounted for.

The video clip had been filmed on someone's phone. It wasn't of great quality but you could make out what was going on and that people were being rescued, just as others were risking their lives saving them.

The report showed a mix of how the site looked like now and what it had been like during the night, and into the early hours of the morning.

In the background Melanie gasped as she saw Joe staggering away from the trailer park carrying a young child in his arms. Firemen followed behind with other children who'd been rescued.

'I hope he didn't go back in,' Melanie said under her breath.

*   *   *

During the course of the morning both Mr David and Mr Peter called into the office and stood with Melanie watching the events of the previous night.

Eva arrived to make sure they had seen 'Joe the hero' as she called him.

Of course, there were many heroes that night.

'Has anyone actually seen him?' Melanie asked, her voice faltering.

Everyone shook their heads.

'He'll be fine. The firemen would have taken over. They'd make sure he left it to the professionals.'

'From what they were saying, they needed him to show them the layout of the site. The smoke was so thick they couldn't see anything. And he knew who lived where and made sure that everyone was accounted for.'

'A hero indeed,' Mr David said. 'Is that one of his challenges?'

It was Eva who brought Melanie a hot sweet tea and told her to go and sit down in Peter's office for a little while until she felt better.

'I can't bear to tear myself away from the screen,' Melanie said.

'Don't worry, we'll let you know if they say anything new. Go on.'

Melanie's hands were shaking as she sipped the warming tea.

'His parents died in a fire,' she whispered and Eva gently stroked her back. 'To say he's brave is an understatement.'

'I just wish I knew he was safe, and Queenie too, of course.'

'The report definitely said they'd got everyone out, and that miraculously there were no fatalities.'

Over the next few days other news stories became the main ones but the fire was not forgotten about.

It soon became clear that it had started because of the build-up of rubbish near the entrance to the site.

The council had been criticised for not doing their duty and collecting it on a regular basis.

There wasn't a separate entrance and exit and all the rubbish was near the entrance. That was possibly where the fire began.

Apparently it had formed a wall between the mobile homes and the rest of the world. The residents had been trapped inside and the fire was blazing before anyone raised the alarm.

Although Melanie hadn't actually seen Joe, Peter Darcy had, and assured her that he and Queenie were as well as could be expected.

'The smoke and the fumes have affected everyone and it has hit them hard emotionally but only a few people were treated for burns.'

We Meet Again

Melanie collected her mother and Anita from the station when they returned from their seaside break. They both looked relaxed and Melanie could tell it had been a great success.

She dropped Anita off and then took her mother back to the retirement home where she lived. Melanie had already been in and stocked up her fridge with fresh milk and bread.

'Do you want me to stay and help you unpack?' she asked.

'I think I'll do that tomorrow. I've had a lovely week, really I have, but the travelling has worn me out. I'm going to have an early night.'

Melanie kissed her mum goodnight and made her way out.

She was surprised and delighted to see Joe in the reception area. Without thinking, she threw her arms around him and gave him a hug and kissed his cheek.

'What's this all about?' he said with his lovely smile.

Melanie realised she'd missed seeing those twinkling blue eyes.

'I'm glad you're safe,' Melanie said quietly. 'How's Queenie?'

'The smoke's affected her chest so they're keeping her in hospital, but she should be out tomorrow. She's in good spirits, despite having lost everything.'

'Not everything?'

'No, but all her treasures. She lost so many things that no-one can replace, but she's got a fighting spirit and she'll rally round. They all will.'

'Were you actually there?'

'I'd been working late at my lodgings. I should have been in bed but something made me go over there. Queenie says I've got a sixth sense. I don't know about that, but it's just as well I did, as I was able to sound the alarm.

'They were all trapped on the other

side of the wall of fire. There was a guy walking his dog — he rang the fire brigade while I started to rescue people.'

Melanie stepped back and looked down at her shoes, suddenly feeling awkward being in his company, standing so close to him. Had she really kissed him?

She could feel him looking at her.

'So, what brings you here?' she asked in a bright and cheery voice. She forced herself to look up into his handsome face.

'I could ask you the same thing,' he said.

'My mum lives here,' Melanie told him.

'And I've been here to speak to the warden about some business,' Joe said.

'I see,' Melanie said. 'You'll need to come into the office again to see Mr Peter.'

'I really can't see the point now,' he replied. 'The events of the last few days have made me realise that money isn't important, it's people that matter.'

'That's true, of course,' Melanie agreed 'but wouldn't it be useful to have some money to help rebuild your lives?'

'If I'm honest, I feel as if I'm a pawn in my grandfather's little game. For whatever reason he didn't visit me when he was alive and now he's got me doing all sorts of pointless exercises. I'm tired of it all.'

'They're not pointless,' Melanie said quickly but she could see that he did look tired. He'd obviously been suffering from shock and should be at home resting.

'Have you eaten?' she asked. 'You look as though you could do with a good meal.'

'I haven't had much appetite lately,' Joe admitted, 'but we could go back to that little Italian restaurant near the gallery.'

'If you're sure,' Melanie said. 'I thought you didn't like it there. We could go elsewhere, perhaps where you'd feel more comfortable?'

'You're right, I didn't like it there, but once I'd been and I'd started to taste a different sort of life, I began to feel I didn't fit in with my old life but I didn't fit in with this new life either. I just don't seem to belong anywhere any more.'

They walked along the river towards the Italian restaurant. The waiter recognised them and showed them to the same table for two as they'd had before.

'It seems ages ago that we were here last and yet it can't have been that long ago. Tell me what's been happening in your life, other than you getting a new haircut?'

Melanie told him how she was coping well at work without Anita, and that she'd not only been offered a pay increase but had been head hunted.

'They've sent through the information and it is tempting, but I like it where I am. Now they are paying me more and offering to train me up on other aspects of law, I think I might stay where I am. It's good to be among people where I feel valued.'

'What about finding your first lot of parents?' Joe asked.

'I have made progress. I think my father died a few years ago but I've made contact with my mother, although she seems more like a stranger at the moment. We've e-mailed each other once or twice but we don't really know anything about one another and I don't feel we've connected.'

'It's hard unless you meet face to face, I suppose.'

'She lives in Ireland.'

'So, visit.'

'There's no chance of that at the moment. I'm needed here, but at least Anita will be back at work in a fortnight, hopefully. My other mother needs me, too, and she's my priority. She's done so much for me over the years.'

'How do you feel about Miss McCree returning? It looked to me as though you were quite happy ruling the roost.'

'I won't deny it. I have enjoyed it and I've made a couple of changes which I hope she'll approve of, but it has made me realise that, although I've been to university, I don't have much practical experience. But I'm learning all the time.'

Their meal came, and for a while they ate in companionable silence.

'And what about you?' Melanie asked after a while. 'Queenie tells me you've moved away.'

'I've been busy, very busy,' he replied after a moment's hesitation.

Melanie wanted to ask if he had a girlfriend and if it was her that was keeping him busy, but she didn't want to know the answer, just in case it was 'Yes'.

What's in a Kiss?

As soon as Anita had her plaster removed and was given the all clear by the hospital, she returned to work.

They had a thunderstorm on Monday afternoon and it was no surprise that Joe appeared, hoping to see Peter Darcy. Joe wouldn't be doing much gardening in this weather.

As soon as Melanie had noticed the dark clouds she had got out his file and was waiting for him to appear. What she hadn't expected was that it wasn't her who was called into the office this time, but Anita.

'But I always go in,' Melanie objected. 'I've been handling this case from the beginning.'

'And now you're not,' Peter Darcy told her firmly. 'Believe me, it's for the best,' he added. 'You haven't done anything wrong. You're just going to have to trust me on this one.'

With that, the door was closed and Melanie could only guess as to what was being discussed. She had never felt so left out before. Everyone knew, without a shadow of a doubt, that Joe had made a huge sacrifice by putting himself at risk and going into the burning site and rescuing his neighbours. It was obvious that he'd achieved that task but she really wanted to know what the next one was.

Nothing was said when they all emerged from the office a short while later. The information had become confidential and Melanie knew not to ask what had been said. Perhaps Joe had requested Anita instead of her? Maybe that's what he'd wanted to discuss with Mr Darcy.

Suddenly the office didn't seem such a great place to be. She wondered if she should have accepted the other job, or perhaps now was the time to up sticks and go visit her other family in Ireland.

For the first time in many weeks, Melanie was glad when it was time to leave the office. She quickly headed over to her mother's. She was deep in thought about what she was going to make them for tea, so she didn't notice Joe at first. He was just about to get into his van.

He stopped and smiled. Melanie returned the smile but hurried on into the building.

She couldn't help noticing the large colourful flower pots at the entrance to the building and the new hanging baskets that were full of trailing petunias. She paused a moment to enjoy them before heading up the stairs to her mother's apartment.

'Have you seen the pretty flowers at the front?' she asked her mother.

'Don't take your shoes off,' came the reply. 'I've got something to show you first.'

With the help of her stick, June led the way along the first floor corridor. A short way down was a door which previously had only been used by the caretaker.

'Are you allowed to go in there?' Melanie asked as her mother pushed it open.

'You must see what he's done,' June said.

The door opened on to a beautiful roof garden.

'How come I've never seen this before?' Melanie said. 'It's beautiful. I thought you said you didn't have any garden here?'

'We didn't, until your friend Joe came along.'

Melanie took a closer look. They were standing on top of the new function hall which had been a fairly recent addition. It had a flat roof and it appeared Joe had now installed a safety rail all the way around, laid decking on the ground, filled the area with brightly coloured pots of flowers and added a few hanging baskets on the outside wall.

There were even a couple of benches where residents could sit and enjoy the little sun trap.

'He said all he did was a bit of weeding and mowing the lawn,' Melanie said. 'I had no idea he was so talented.'

They walked to the edge of the roof garden and looked out over the car park. Joe had brightened up the place with hanging baskets, bringing colour to the drab concrete building.

Melanie recalled he'd been speaking with the manager when she'd seen him here.

'What do you think?' Joe asked as he appeared in the doorway.

'Oh, Joe — it's beautiful and such a good use of space. I can't believe no-one did it years ago when the hall was first built.'

'We had to check that it would be safe to walk on, but we got the go ahead, and I'm pleased with it. What about you?' This last question was aimed at June.

'I can't tell you how many times I've said to Melanie that the only thing this place lacks is a garden, and now you've

148

given us just that. Thank you so much. I do hope you're going to be able to come and keep it looking nice for us?'

'I'll pop in now and again and check on it, but I'm hoping the residents will water the plants.' Joe smiled.

'That's the least we can do,' June said.

'Is it something I can be proud of?' Joe asked Melanie. He was looking very serious.

'I'd certainly be proud if I'd done this,' Melanie said, and then the penny dropped. His task must have been to do something he was proud of, or something for the community. 'I'll take some photos to show Mr Darcy what you've done.'

'In that case I'll be in tomorrow to see him again.'

'I don't think rain is forecast,' Melanie told him.

'I just want to crack on and get this over with,' he said and Melanie felt as though he was saying that he'd be glad when he had no reason to come and visit them any more.

Perhaps he had plans to move away, once he'd received his grandfather's inheritance?

★ ★ ★

The following afternoon Anita, Melanie and both the Darcy brothers were in the front office discussing how to rearrange the desks to accommodate more filing cabinets.

Over the weekend the two brothers had been in the attic, for reasons known only to themselves, and they had brought down loads of old files which now needed to be stored safely away.

They'd tried one idea but it was proving too tight to make it practical. Anita had suggested she made a pot of tea, while they decided what might work better.

As she was doing so, Peter Darcy and Melanie stood by the window watching the world go by.

They both noticed Joe Davies in the

distance. He seemed to be heading in their direction. There was a zebra crossing and a woman trying to manage a pushchair, two bulging bags of shopping and a small dog.

Melanie watched Joe speak to the woman. The woman looked him up and down. She then looked at the pushchair, the grocery bags and the dog.

She appeared to come to a decision and handed Joe the shopping bags which he carried across the road and then went out of sight with the woman following alongside. Darcy aloud wondered if he'd taken them further down the road to the multi-storey car park.

'Tea,' Anita said, placing a tray of mugs on the table with a plate of chocolate biscuits.

'We could use that desk over there as a reception desk in order to greet clients when they come in and then move that one into the corner,' Melanie suggested. 'It might be a bit dark over there but quieter for making phone calls.'

'I like that idea,' Anita said. 'I've often thought we should have a reception desk.'

'Are you going to tell us we also need a receptionist?' David Darcy asked.

Melanie looked at Anita.

'I think we could probably take it in turns, depending on whether we're working on the computer or having to make lots of calls. What do you think?'

'It's worth a try,' Melanie agreed.

They were in the middle of moving the furniture round once more, when Joe arrived, having done one good deed for the day. Without a second thought he discarded his jacket and rolled up his sleeves to help move both the tables into place.

'Sorry, we're in a bit of a pickle this afternoon,' Peter Darcy apologised.

'Don't worry, I don't think my tasks need to be kept particularly confidential, unless you know what's coming next?'

'Actually I do,' Peter said. 'Your task was to assist a stranger but it looked to me as though I have just witnessed that from my position near the window. Don't you agree, Melanie? We saw you help that woman with her bags of shopping. So we can move straight on to the next one.'

Melanie nodded and handed him the file and he found the envelope marked number nine.

'Ah,' he said, 'you are required to do something out of character. I do wish Mr Huntley had thought about how we're supposed to prove what is in your character and what is not.'

'I'm sure you'll think of something,' Anita said. 'Now, let's get this office straight so we can get on with our work.'

'Yes, boss,' David Darcy said and everyone laughed.

Joe's phone buzzed.

'More work!' he said, gave them a wave, and disappeared as quickly as he'd appeared.

'If he'd hung around and chatted for five minutes,' Melanie said, 'that would have been out of character.'

He'd only been gone a minute when Melanie noticed his jacket. She grabbed it and ran to the door. In the distance she could see him, head and shoulders above the rest of the crowd. She hugged the jacket to her, and headed off after him, running as fast as her work shoes would allow.

'Joe, Joe!' she called.

It wasn't until she was almost able to reach out and touch him that he obviously heard his name and turned round.

She was out of breath but managed to hold up his jacket. He treated her to one of his beaming smiles.

'Thank you,' he said. 'I wouldn't have got very far. My car keys are in the pocket.'

They were standing on the pavement near an empty building. It was the quieter end of town near the car-parking areas. Melanie thought he was about to say something.

He took his coat from her, giving her

a moment more to get her breath, then pulled her into his arms and before she knew it, his lips had descended on hers.

Joe had full lips which were warm and soft. His kiss was gentle. It was tender, as though he'd kissed her many times.

It was all over so quickly. Joe stepped back and looked into Melanie's wide eyes.

'I'm sorry,' he said. 'I had to do something out of character.'

'Oh,' Melanie said, suddenly feeling deflated. 'You were trying to cross another thing off your list. Was that all?'

'Actually, it's something I've wanted to do since I first met you but I didn't think it was right.'

'Well, now you can come back and tell my boss, and embarrass me in front of the whole office, and get on to your next challenge.

'Don't worry, you've only got three more to do, then you can take your money and you won't ever have to see us again.'

Joe looked taken aback.

'Is that what you want?' he asked.

'Of course! I don't want to be made a laughing stock!'

'I can't guarantee Mr Darcy will believe me without seeing it for himself so, with your permission, I'll have to catch you off guard again.'

'I'm sure you can think of a much better way to fulfil your task.'

Joe looked up as though he was searching for inspiration. He smiled again but this time it was more of a grin.

'No,' he said. 'I can't think of any better way. Shall we head back to your office?'

Despite herself, Melanie could feel the colour rising up in her cheeks.

'I'm teasing,' Joe said.

He turned to go.

'Thanks for bringing my jacket.'

Melanie watched him amble down the street. She was cross with him, confused by him and also more than a little disappointed.

So Many Questions

Melanie made her way back to the office, taking her time and fanning herself so that if she still had red cheeks she could blame it on her running.

Everyone was involved in straightening out the furniture by the time she returned and no-one made any comment.

'Are we going to keep it like this for a while?' she asked, itching to tidy up so she could get on with her work.

She liked to reach the end of each day feeling she'd achieved something and she knew one of her house-buying clients was waiting for a report.

It took another hour before she felt they were organised again. She sat down gratefully and quickly made a few phone calls to her clients.

Peter Darcy had noticed his door was no longer sticking.

'Oh, Joe did that the other day. I thought you'd asked him to.'

'I didn't. Did he leave an invoice?'

'No. I think he was just being helpful, you know Joe.'

'I am beginning to get to know him. I wish his grandfather was here to see what a fine young man he's growing into.'

As they were speaking Melanie became aware of Mr Peter's attention being distracted. He seemed to have seen something behind her. She turned and saw Joe with a huge bouquet of flowers.

'These are for you.' He leaned closer to Melanie for another kiss on her lips.

Again he was gentle but she could sense the passion in the way he cupped her face toward his.

'I hope I haven't embarrassed you again,' he said and then looked up at Anita and the Darcy brothers.

'I hope Miss Harper will forgive me, but we all know I had to do something out of character. I'd be happy to repeat it, if you missed it,' he said and everyone laughed.

Melanie's heart was beating quickly but she wasn't going to show him how she felt.

'I'll just put these in water,' she said, flustered, 'and then I'll get your file for Mr Darcy.'

Once again it was Anita who was called into the office. Melanie got on with rearranging the things on her desk so they were all to hand and just as she wanted them.

The three of them were still talking as they emerged from the office. No other clients were about.

'At least this one is straightforward, but how can I prove I have spoken to someone I haven't spoken to in years?'

'Melanie can type a quick letter for you, and you can ask the person to sign it, or if they refuse, then you could ask a witness.'

Melanie did as she was asked. Peter Darcy nodded his approval as she printed off a copy and gave it to Joe.

'I've given you two copies just in case you have to repeat the exercise.'

'Don't you have any confidence in me?' he asked with a glint of humour in his eyes.

'I have every confidence in you, but you can never tell how someone will react if you haven't spoken to them in many years, and you can't guarantee you'll have a third party around to verify what's gone on.'

'I suppose you may have something there,' he conceded.

'Have you got an idea of whom you'll speak to?' Melanie asked.

She looked at Joe with his large hands and wondered how he managed to pick out the small weeds when he was gardening.

'You remember I told you Queenie had arranged a girl for me to marry?'

Melanie swallowed hard and wondered why she felt so uncomfortable. She knew she liked Joe. He was such an easy person to get on with.

But did she like him that much? Was

she experiencing feelings of jealousy?

'Yes, I recall you saying something about how it all went wrong and you were deemed to be cursed.'

'She'd met a boy at school and had fallen for him. Her parents wanted her to marry one of us, a traveller, and Queenie wanted me to marry within our group as the parents came to an agreement. I was happy to go along with it, but she was not.'

'Doesn't love come into any of this?' Melanie found herself asking.

'I'm sure we would have grown to love each other. We vaguely knew each other and didn't dislike one another, it was just that she'd met this other boy and thought she loved him.'

'And you're going to speak to her?' Melanie asked. 'Did she ever marry the other boy?'

'They ran away together and got married without either family knowing. No-one knew where she was for a while. I think it took a long time before either family would forgive them but now they have two little girls and everything has sorted itself out for the best for them.'

'So you think she'll want to speak to you?'

'It's not her I'm going to speak to,' Joe said. 'Her mother blamed me, for some reason. I don't think there was anything logical about it, but she needed to point the finger at someone, and it was me.

'That's why she made up the story that I was cursed. These things have a habit of sticking and she could have done a lot of damage. I have no issues with her and I want to make peace with her.' Joe leaned on her desk.

'It's not really for me,' he continued. 'I don't believe in curses. I understand what really happened, but Queenie took it very badly. She felt she ought to do her best for me, for the sake of my mother, and she felt she'd let my parents down when the wedding plans fell apart.'

Melanie looked up at Joe. Even in the

dark corner of the office his blue eyes seemed to twinkle.

'Then I'd better wish you good luck.'

'I wondered . . . ' Joe hesitated. 'I know it's not part of your remit, but could I buy you dinner afterwards?'

'Me?'

'I don't want her to think I am being nice to her so that I can get to see her daughter again. We all know that would cause trouble. I thought if you were with me, and I explained I just want to close the matter and make Queenie feel better, she'd be more likely to let me speak.'

Melanie thought about what he was saying and could see the sense in it.

'Why don't you ask Queenie?'

'I could do,' Joe said, 'but to be honest it could all go horribly wrong and that won't help, and my grandmother still isn't fully recovered from the shock of the fire.'

'I thought she was out of hospital.'

'She is, and the council have given her a lovely new mobile home. She's got everything she needs, but she's frail and all she really wants is to see me settled.'

The local council, while not admitting liability for the fire, had provided a large plot of land and, working with Joe and the travelling community, they had assembled a few mobile homes.

Not all the families were rehoused together. Some people had gone to stay with family, some had moved away or taken to the road again.

'I don't know if I can do this,' Melanie said. 'I don't know if it would be professional of me, and I do have my own mother to care for.'

'Of course,' Joe said, 'but I did want to ask. Please think about it. I could ask Mr Darcy if you could have the afternoon off to come with me, but I think you all have spent a lot of time on my grandfather's will already and I can't ask for more.'

'Did you know both the Darcy brothers knew him?'

'I knew Peter did. I think he told me

they were at school together,' Joe said. 'One day I'd like to ask Peter to tell me more about him, but he always seems so busy. He looks like a man with a lot on his mind.'

Melanie watched as Joe picked up his belongings. He had a sad look in his eyes once again, which she could identify with. She didn't know anyone who was truly related to her and, although he knew Queenie and had loads of aunts, uncles and cousins, he didn't know his parents and had no siblings.

'OK,' Melanie said. 'I will come with you — but it'll have to be an evening after work when Mum has got some company.'

'That's a deal,' Joe said. 'Will you contact me?'

'I will.'

★   ★   ★

That evening when Melanie eventually got back to her room, she switched on her laptop and checked her e-mails. There were two from Bridget O'Mally.

One was full of news. It consisted of incidents that had happened in the tiny village and the reactions of family members. Bridget wrote as though Melanie knew them all, but of course she hadn't a clue.

The second e-mail was brief, but full of love. Bridget said again and again how much she loved her daughter. She gave no reason why she'd then decided to have her adopted. Melanie still wasn't sure she'd found the right person.

Melanie read both e-mails through once more. They left her cold. The first one was like watching an episode of a soap opera that was in series three and you had never watched it before, or read the blurb.

The second one just threw up so many questions. If she was so loved, then why had she been brought up in a different country by two complete strangers? It was not the sort of question you could ask via e-mail, but did she really want to meet this woman?

Not for the first time, Melanie wondered if she was related to Bridget at all. She looked at Bridget's Facebook photo and wondered if she would look like that in years to come.

Melanie e-mailed Bridget saying she was available to Skype if now was a good time. Almost immediately her screen pulsated as the call came through. She hesitated over the 'answer' button, wondering if she was doing the right thing.

'I'll never know unless I do it,' she told herself and pressed the button.

Bridget had aged since her photograph had been taken. Her auburn hair was more like salt and pepper and she'd put on weight. But Melanie liked to think she could still see a likeness between this stranger and herself.

Bridget liked to talk. Melanie let her because initially she found her strong Irish accent hard to follow, but gradually she became tuned in, and the more she listened, the easier it was to follow.

A couple of times she tried to

interrupt with a question and then to try and ask specifically why she was adopted, but either Bridget did not hear her, or there was a slight time delay on Skype that prevented a proper two-way conversation. After a while, Melanie waved at the woman and told her she had to go, but would call again.

Melanie got ready for bed, but knew she wouldn't be able to get to sleep for a while. She heard Anita switch off the news and climb up the wooden stairs.

She lay in bed for some time before getting up and looking for a notepad and pen, She wrote down all her unanswered questions and things she would like to ask her mother, if only she could. She felt better once she'd committed them to paper.

A Difficult Encounter

The following morning over breakfast, Anita said she'd promised to go and visit June. They were going to plan another trip away together and they were considering about going to the cinema one evening if it wasn't too late.

Melanie was delighted the two women enjoyed each other's company and had found so many shared interests.

She texted Joe to say she would be available tonight if he wanted to go and speak to the mother of the girl he might have married.

The day flew by, but it wasn't a satisfying one. She'd been very busy all the time but didn't feel she had achieved very much.

It felt strange after work, with Anita going one way to visit her mother, and Melanie heading back to her lodgings.

Once home, she changed and freshened

up. Carefully she applied a little make-up and was just putting on her lipstick when there was a knock at the door.

Joe looked as handsome as ever. He wore denim trousers and an air-force blue shirt.

'It's a bit of a drive, I'm afraid,' Joe said, 'but I've borrowed my uncle's car. It's more comfortable than the van.'

'Do you need me to navigate?'

'Don't worry, I'm pretty sure I know where I'm going. I just don't know what to expect when I get there.'

It was a warm evening. Melanie was very much aware of Joe sitting beside her. He was more talkative than she'd ever known him. He chatted about his childhood with Queenie and his early memories of playing football with his cousins.

'Are you nervous?' Melanie asked after a while.

'Is it so obvious?' he asked with a little laugh. 'I thought this one would be easy but now we're on our way I'm really frightened that she'll just slam the door in my face.'

'Does she know you're coming?'

'No. I've got no way of contacting her. Queenie seemed to think it was probably better that way.'

At last they pulled into a caravan site. Lights were on in some of the vans. Dogs roamed about and some children played football just as Joe had done when he was a child.

'What do you want me to do?' Melanie asked.

'Just come with me,' Joe said. 'I'll do the talking.'

Joe walked up to a van and knocked on the door. A small child answered and Joe said something. Melanie wasn't sure if they were talking another language or whether she'd misheard.

A few moments later, a stocky woman appeared. She had long dark hair and an apron. It was clear she recognised Joe straightaway.

'What do you want?'

'I only want to clear the air. There's bad blood between our families and I want to sort it out.'

'I've got nothing to say to you, Robbie-Joe. Leave me alone. Leave my family alone.' With that she slammed the door as he had feared.

He looked down at his feet. Melanie reached out for his arm.

'At least you tried,' she said, 'and technically you did speak to her.'

Joe turned to Melanie with a look of thunder on his handsome face.

'You still don't understand, do you? It's not all about playing my grandfather's silly game. I'm doing this for Queenie. She's coming to the end of her life and it pains her to live with the conflict and friction. She just wants them to recognise I wasn't the guilty party, nor was she, and it was all a long time ago.'

'And I suppose it's all turned out right in the end,' Melanie said quietly, as she did her best to understand Joe's family problems.

'You might think so, but my grandmother certainly does not.'

'Then you are right, Joe Davies, I do

not understand.'

They slowly started to walk back to the car. Melanie could sense Joe was uncomfortable. He put his hands in his pockets then took them out again. He took a deep breath.

'My culture is all about families. You are born into a family. You grow up with lots of brothers and sisters. You marry early, probably a cousin or some other relation. Everyone knows everyone else. It's a very close-knit existence.'

'I can see that, but . . . '

'Ten years ago I should have been married. Tara was. I wasn't. Although it was her who had broken the rules, she did the right thing by getting married and has since started a family. Whereas here am I, ten years older, and unmarried.'

'But you're still young.'

'I'm thirty and believe me it's hard. The men I mix with all have a wife and several children. I have nothing in common with them. I envy them and sometimes, ironically, they envy me.'

'Can't you just mix with other unmarried men?'

'There aren't any, not in my culture. We marry and we marry for life. I don't know anyone who has ever divorced. It just doesn't happen. I'm not saying that everyone lives happily ever after, but we do make the best of it, and generally it works.'

'I am beginning to see.'

'Queenie did try to arrange other marriages for me but with the curse hanging over me and the bad feeling, no-one wanted to know. It wasn't anything against me. There are always other men, with no history, for a young girl to turn to and so they do, and no-one wants a thirty-year-old. The girls now think I'm ancient.'

'So that's why it's so important to sort this out and break the cycle?'

'Yes. Although now I wish I'd done it years ago.'

'You still here?' a woman's voice said. She sounded as though she was used to being in control.

'Nancy, please just hear me out,' Joe said. 'It's been ten years since Tara said she'd chosen to marry someone else. It wasn't her fault, it wasn't mine, and it certainly wasn't Queenie's. I'm not asking for anything, just that we can shake hands and forget the bad blood.'

'I heard there was a fire,' Nancy said.

'Yeah, the whole site was destroyed, but no-one hurt.'

'And Queenie's OK?'

'She's taken it hard. Her chest is bad but you know Queenie, she never complains. The worst thing is,' Joe hesitated and swallowed hard, 'the community have been split up. Not on purpose, but that's what's happened, and she doesn't like change, not at her age.'

Nancy seemed to notice Melanie for the first time. She'd tried to stay behind Joe and keep in the shadows. Joe lived in a different world. Melanie could see that clearly now. Nancy looked her up and down and then back at Joe.

She said something to Joe that Melanie definitely didn't understand, but Joe did and replied. He then reverted to English.

'You sure you don't want anything?' Nancy asked suspiciously.

'Queenie's not well. I'm trying to put her affairs in order and make peace where we can.' He held out his hand.

Nancy looked down at it. Someone called her from inside the van. She shook Joe's hand.

'Thank you. No hard feelings?'

'No hard feelings,' Nancy agreed.

'I'll be off, then,' Joe said. He reached out and took Melanie's hand and led her back to the car. His hand was warm but he was shaking.

Back inside the car Melanie touched his arm, giving it a little squeeze.

'Are you all right? Do you want a minute before we drive back?'

'I wanted her to say I was no longer cursed,' Joe admitted.

'Was it her who cursed you because she felt you'd let her daughter down?'

'Something like that.' Joe shrugged. 'Queenie took it so hard because she felt she had a duty to sort things out, as my mother would have done. She's had a hard life, you know.'

'Queenie?'

'Yes. It was her sister who ran away with my grandfather, Robert Huntley. Queenie had been told she must never speak to her again, but I think they did keep in touch, though Queenie was scared her father would find out.

'Then, her sister died in childbirth and she took it hard, but Robert worked abroad by all accounts, and couldn't look after his daughter, Annie. Queenie's children were mainly grown up and married, although she did still have one son at home. She brought up Annie and her son and eventually they married. That was my mum and dad.'

'So she lost a son in that fire?' Melanie said, making the connection. Joe nodded. 'She's never really come to terms with that but I suppose she's always treated me more like her son than her grandson. I am like my father, she says.'

Melanie gave Joe's arm another squeeze.

'It must have been so awful to lose them. She's had such a lot of tragedy in her life. No wonder she's so worried about losing you, too.'

'She's worried?' Joe asked in surprise. 'Why would she be worried about losing me?'

Melanie took a deep sigh and cleared her throat before answering.

'Well firstly, she thinks that once you have the inheritance from your grandfather then you might up and leave. According to her, you've more or less left her home anyway.'

'Is that what she thinks?' Joe said, almost to himself. 'I've tried to explain to her what I have to do, but she is so set in her ways and she's never liked change.

'It seems whatever I do, I can't please everyone.'

One of Those Days

The rain started while Melanie was on her way to work and got heavier. A car drove past and sent a cold puddle of water up on to the pavement which drenched her feet and ankles. She shivered and squelched along, hurrying to get to the office.

Everyone was in a hurry. The streets were busier than normal and even though she had left early she arrived a little late for work. It was the first time this had happened, but Peter Darcy was waiting for her. She noticed him glance at his watch.

'Can we have a word in my office?' he said.

Melanie had wanted to discard her wet shoes and dry herself off with the hand drier in the cloakroom, but Mr Darcy was waiting.

'Sit down,' he said as he opened a file

on his desk. 'You have been with us some time now. I realise I should have done a six-month review with you but I think it coincided with Anita being off and it was a very busy time.'

Melanie nodded. She was feeling uncomfortable and it had nothing to do with her wet feet.

'I gather from Miss McCree that you did not feel you were suited to the conveyancing side of our business?'

'It is a bit boring, and very stressful for everyone concerned, including me, and that's all I was doing in the beginning.'

'It's a shame you felt like that. I do understand, but in order to be successful, you need to know all aspects of the firm and to have experience in various different areas. Besides, if you don't do the conveyancing, who else would do it?'

'I realise that, but that wasn't what I signed up to do. I don't think I'd reach my potential if I were just sorting out people's house sales.'

'And is there a direction you see your career going in?' he asked.

Melanie wondered if he was going to ask her which course she'd like to go on.

'We're a small, family firm and we need people who can turn their hand to whatever the task is that needs doing. Do you see where I'm going?'

'I'm not sure,' Melanie said. She hoped it wasn't going to be bad news.

'You're a young lady with lots of ambition. Have you a career plan in mind?'

'Not as such,' Melanie replied. 'I want to try to have a go at all sorts of things. I did manage the office when Anita was off.'

'And you did a very good job then. I'm wondering where we go from here.'

'What are you getting at, Mr Darcy?' she asked.

'I am wondering if you feel this is the right job for you?' He stopped and put up his hand. 'Think about it. There are big companies out there that would be able to offer you more than we can. I mean in terms of experience as well as the sort of pay they can give.'

'Are you trying to get rid of me?' Melanie asked.

'No, but we are looking at ways of restructuring the office and I'm wondering where you see yourself in, say, five years' time or even in one year?'

Melanie was relieved when the phone rang and she was able to escape from his office.

It was as if her whole world was being turned upside-down. She liked her job now, although knew she had more to offer. She thought she was perfectly content helping June most evenings after work but now, should she make more of an effort to get to know her birth mother?

At the moment there seemed more than the Irish Sea between them.

And then there was Joe. She liked him. She thought he liked her but there was no denying they came from different backgrounds, different cultures. Would this stand in their way?

★   ★   ★

Melanie signed the letter to say that she'd been witness to Joe talking with Nancy. Listening to their strained conversation, it sounded to her as though they had not met, let alone spoken to each other, in at least ten years, as Joe had said.

'You probably think you've done this already,' Peter Darcy said to Joe. 'But your eleventh task is to perform a brave act.'

'Doesn't the fire count?' Melanie asked.

'I'm afraid not. That was in the past.'

Joe nodded and looked very grave. Melanie wondered if he was thinking back to that dreadful night when he had to risk his own life to save his neighbours. Even she could almost smell the smoke just by thinking of it.

'You're nearly there,' Peter Darcy told Joe. 'I'm sure we'll see you again when you have completed this one. We will need to be able to prove it. Don't forget that.'

Joe nodded and shook Mr Darcy's hand.

'Will you come for a drink with me?' Joe asked Melanie. 'I think there's something we need to talk about.'

Melanie didn't know how to answer him. Peter Darcy was standing close by. He was leaning over Anita's desk signing a series of letters she'd typed up for him. Melanie suspected he could hear what was being said wherever she chose to stand in the office.

Melanie sat at her desk but thought about her life. Was Joe asking her out just so he could rescue her from a runaway car and therefore add another brave act to his list?

She was about to accept his offer of a drink, but on her terms. She would ask him to work around her duties as a daughter. She stood and gestured him to the front door where they could stand in the porch and not be overheard.

She thought it would be useful to speak with Joe about Bridget O'Mally and what her next step would be. She was just about to speak when she noticed Joe check his watch. He'd already done so twice in the last few minutes.

'Do you have an urgent appointment?' she asked.

'I do.' He nodded.

'Well, don't let me keep you,' Melanie snapped. She showed Joe out of the door without giving him an answer.

As she returned to her desk she saw that both the Darcy brothers were getting ready to go out. Hurriedly she fetched the relevant files for them.

'Don't make any new appointments for the rest of the day,' Peter said, who was going to be in court. 'I may see you this evening. If not, we can catch up in the morning.'

There was a different atmosphere once the two men had gone. Melanie sat back and composed herself.

She was startled when Anita brought her over a cup of tea and a box of tissues.

'Do you want to talk?' she offered as she hovered near the desk.

'Why is everything so complicated?' Melanie asked.

'Is it?'

'When I came here, I thought I knew everything there was to know about the law but now I realise I've hardly scratched the surface. I thought I was content just knowing my adoptive parents, but now I'm intrigued to know more about my roots. Although I thought I'd make an instant connection with my 'real' mother, I haven't. Her life seems so alien to me.'

Melanie sipped her hot, sweet tea and sniffed.

'And then there's Joe.'

'Yes — Joe,' Anita echoed. 'That seems to be going well, at least.'

Melanie looked up in surprise.

'It's good to have a friend,' she said, 'and I'm sure he's the sort of person I could ask to do anything, and he would if he could.'

'But?'

186

'I know we're so different in many ways, and I know he's only a friend, so why do I feel so possessive when he rushes off for another appointment or is cagey about where he's living? And heaven knows what's been keeping him so busy these last few months.'

'Have you spoken to him about all this?'

'No, of course not. It's none of my business.'

'Didn't I hear him ask you out for a drink?' Anita asked with a little smile. 'Perhaps he wants to get to know you better.'

'I didn't give him an answer,' Melanie said.

'You could call him.'

'Is that what you would do, Anita?'

Melanie wiped her eyes and finished her tea. She called Joe but there was no reply.

'Oh, well,' she said, putting on a brave face. 'I'll try again later.'

During the course of the afternoon she tried to get hold of him a couple more times but without luck.

'I wonder how they're getting on this afternoon?' Anita said.

'Who?'

Anita didn't answer. Melanie looked up and saw a strange expression on her face.

'Is something going on?' Melanie asked.

'I've said too much already,'

'But you haven't said a word. Now I know something is up. They're not in court, are they?'

Melanie watched Anita but she did her best to avoid eye contact.

The two women hardly spoke for the rest of the afternoon. Melanie tried to contact Joe a few more times but there was still no reply.

'It's just as well I'm not offering him lots of gardening business,' Melanie muttered, 'because he'd be missing out.'

★   ★   ★

For once they were both ready to leave dead on five-thirty. Melanie hurried along to her mother's where she prepared tea.

'Are you OK?' she asked her mum. 'You're very quiet tonight and you've hardly eaten a thing.'

'I didn't sleep well,' June admitted, 'and I've been fighting the tiredness all day. The last thing I wanted to do was to have an afternoon nap. That would mean that I wouldn't sleep tonight and it would become a vicious circle.'

'I suppose it won't harm to have an early night,' Melanie suggested. 'Do you want the radio on or shall I read to you?'

'Is it me or has the weather chilled down?' June asked.

'It is cooler tonight,' Melanie agreed. 'Do you need a rug?'

'I think I'll have a hot bath. That'll warm me up and help me sleep, too. Will you run it for me?'

Melanie spent the next half hour preparing the bathroom with fresh towels and clearing away the tea things.

'I don't know what I'd do without you,' June said. 'I know I don't tell you often enough, but I do appreciate what you do. I've been thinking . . . '

'What?'

'I could get a carer in so that you wouldn't have to come over straight from work. I know it makes such a long day for you.'

'It's no problem, and I haven't anything else to do.'

'But that's it, you should do. A girl of your age ought to be out with her friends meeting people, dancing and romancing.'

'I do occasionally meet up with people from university but we're all busy with work and one or two have got married.'

'Just remember we've had this conversation,' June said, 'so that if you are invited out you know I can manage and you don't have to worry about me.'

'Thanks for the thought, but I've no plans to get a social life just now.'

As she spoke, the beeping noise of her phone came from her bag.

'Of course, that could be an invitation to a party,' Melanie laughed, 'but it's more likely to be Anita asking if I'll need any supper when I get in.'

'Is her arm completely healed now?' June asked.

'Oh, yes, she's fine but I think she's seriously thinking of retiring very soon. She hasn't said anything definite but it keeps creeping into the conversation.'

'Do you think she'll marry Peter?'

'Pardon?'

'Those two have been friends for years but they are both married to their jobs. I've been thinking for a while that they'll both be lost once they give up work. I wouldn't be surprised if they got together.'

'All they've got in common is crime novels,' Melanie said as she wiped down the work surfaces. 'Right, I'm done now. Do you want me to wait while you get into the bath?'

'I'm fine. We're so well equipped with

rubber mats and grab handles. Off you go.'

Melanie kissed her mother goodnight and made for the lift. As she did so she checked her phone.

To her surprise it was Joe who'd rung. Melanie smiled.

'Well, it served him right that I didn't answer. He never answers my calls,' she muttered.

Her phone beeped again. This time it was a text.

Meet me on the roof garden. Joe.

Melanie paused. He had never sent her a text before. Maybe someone else had typed it for him . . .

It wasn't only June who was tired; she was, too. But Joe was her friend and one of the things she liked about him was that he was always in a cheerful mood. Of course there were times when he was cross but it never lasted long. He'd bounce back and smile again.

She made her way along the corridor. The door to the roof garden was ajar but it would be dark outside. She doubted any of the residents would be using it.

She pushed the door and gasped. It was like a magical grotto. Lots of little fairy lights shone brightly. There was a lantern on the coffee table near the chairs and several garlands of white twinkling lights had been hung above the railings.

Joe emerged from the shadows.

'I've saved us a table for two,' he said although there was no-one else about. 'I thought you'd be walking, so I've poured you a glass of wine.'

'What a wonderful idea.' Melanie laughed. She felt her shoulders relax before she'd even sipped the warming red wine.

'It's so beautiful up here, even in the dark.'

'I thought there would be more moonlight tonight,' Joe said, looking up at the sky, 'but it's too cloudy.'

'Cheers.' They clinked their glasses together. 'You led me to believe you didn't do much garden design,' Melanie said. 'But you've really got a knack for it.'

'I'd like to do more but everything is so busy now. I'm thinking of taking on an apprentice.'

'Really? That's excellent news,' Melanie said, raising her glass. 'Will it be one of your nephews — or maybe a niece?' she added.

'It ought to be,' Joe agreed, 'but a friend of mine has a son who would be perfect.'

Melanie looked at him. It was the way he said, 'a friend of mine'. It sounded as though the friend was very special. She felt her shoulders tense again.

'He's got Downs Syndrome,' Joe continued. 'I don't suppose he'll ever take the initiative but once I've shown him what to do and explained why we do it, he's very reliable.'

'So, business is going well,' Melanie said slowly as she sipped her wine. 'I thought it must be, because you always seem to have appointments to make and you never answer your phone.'

She saw Joe shift awkwardly in his chair.

'I can explain,' he said. 'In fact that's one of the reasons I . . . '

They both heard it at the same time. The noise sounded like a bang and then a cry. In an instant they were up and heading back to the corridor. A man was lying on the floor with his stick beside him and a bag near his feet.

'Stay there,' Joe said. 'Just relax. There's no need to get up until you're ready.'

Melanie rushed to his side.

'It's Mr Picard, isn't it?' The man nodded. 'I'm Melanie Harper, June's daughter, and this is Joe, the man who's done all the lovely hanging baskets and created the roof garden.'

Mr Picard sat up and brushed himself down.

'I've just been to the corner shop,' he said, glancing at the carrier bag. 'I don't know what happened. One minute I was standing. I thought I'd heard voices

— that must have been you two — and then, next thing I knew, I was on the floor looking like a right fool.'

'It doesn't seem as though you've hurt yourself,' Melanie said. 'Can we help you up?'

Between them they managed to get Mr Picard to his feet.

'I'll walk you to your room,' Joe offered.

'If you take my shopping, that would be good. I suppose I ought to think about getting one of those trolleys.'

'I've left Mum in the bath,' Melanie said. 'I'm sure she'll be fine, but I'll just go and check.'

They went their separate ways. By the time Melanie left, having shared a hot chocolate with her mum, there was no sign of Mr Picard and the warden on reception told her that Mr Davies had left about 10 minutes beforehand. He'd had a meeting to attend.

Cool Atmosphere

The following day there was a cloud hanging over the office. Anita had been worried that Melanie was going to say something to Mr Darcy about their conversation the previous day, dropping Anita in it for hinting that all was not as it should be.

Melanie had quietly got on with her work. She had several jobs she wanted to tie up before the end of the week. She consoled herself that it was satisfying to see the purchase or the sale of a property right through to the end and to celebrate once the keys and the money had changed hands.

'I'm nipping out to buy some lunch,' Melanie announced. She'd been hungry and had eaten her sandwiches about 11 o'clock. She was eager to get some fresh air.

Summer had more or less come to an

end. The nights were beginning to draw in and there was definitely a feel of autumn in the air.

Huge cobwebs appeared on the lamp-posts and the path home was littered with horse-chestnut leaves and conkers.

Melanie looked at the shiny conkers and wondered if Queenie was right. Did they mean a good omen?

Melanie bought herself a coffee and a muffin and as it was dry decided to walk to the park to eat it there before returning to the office. She wondered what the atmosphere was going to be like that afternoon.

On her way to the park she heard the distant cries of schoolchildren enjoying their lunch break. She sat by the duck pond sipping the strong black coffee and enjoying each bite of her blueberry muffin. The ducks squawked hopefully but she was oblivious.

Once she came out of her trance she realised the school children had gone in and everywhere was quiet. She checked her watch but she still had time left.

As it was turning into a beautiful afternoon she decided to do a quick circuit of the park before returning to the office and tackling another pile of files.

As she walked past the fence that backed on to the school playground she noticed Joe's van in the car park. Assuming he must be working on their grounds she looked around to see if she could see him.

She was reminded of their brief encounter yesterday. For all she knew their wine glasses were still on the table in the roof garden.

'Is Mr Davies — Joe Davies the gardener — on site?' she asked at reception. 'I won't stop him working, I just want a very quick word.'

Melanie had decided to let him know she could meet him again this evening after she had visited her mother.

'He's in the hall but he's already started, I'm afraid.'

'Started?'

'You're welcome to watch if you

want. Use that door,' the receptionist said as she pointed to a small door leading into the school hall. 'You'll be able to stand at the back without interrupting.'

Melanie hesitated. She knew she ought to get back to the office but she couldn't deny she was intrigued as to what it was Joe was up to now.

She gently pushed open the door. The hall was packed with children sitting on the floor but you couldn't hear a sound other than Joe's lilting voice as he read from a large book.

Melanie was mesmerised for a moment by the scene. He'd certainly captured his audience. There was no doubt about it.

It was only then that she looked again. But he said he could barely read, she thought. She was sure that was what he'd said, and yet here he was reading stories to schoolchildren. She was certain she had not been mistaken, which could only mean he'd lied to her.

And if he'd lied about that, then what other lies had he told her?

Later that evening as Melanie was leaving her mother's apartment she bumped into Joe near the lift.

'Shall we continue where we left off last night?' he asked.

'You lied to me,' Melanie said.

Joe looked surprised.

'You told me . . . '

Melanie stopped as Mr Picard walked slowly along the corridor on his way to the corner shop. She smiled sweetly and the three of them pleasantly passed the time of day.

However, once Mr Picard was in the lift, Joe stepped forward, took Melanie by the crook of the arm and walked her back to the relative privacy of the roof garden.

Once again it was magically lit. She noticed the glasses and the wine and guessed he must have planned to meet her there again.

'Go on,' he said as he took a seat and began to pour their wine.

'You told me you could barely read and yet I saw you, in a school, reading out a story to a room full of children.'

Joe gave a heavy sigh.

'I have been trying to tell you,' he said. He sipped his wine. 'When we first met, it was true I could hardly read. I missed a lot of school because we were travelling around. We'd only stay in one place for a couple of weeks at the most.

'Then, because I was tall and strong, I was picked to work with the men. We worked outside tarmacking drives, chopping down trees. I know I should have been in school but I was learning different skills, practical ones.'

'And you expect me to believe that from the time we first met in the spring when you couldn't swim and you couldn't read, now, suddenly, you've learned to swim and you're confident enough to sit in front of loads of kids and read them a story?'

'If you'd have told me I'd be doing either of those things six months ago, I wouldn't have believed you either, but I can assure you I've changed. I may not have been to university but I'm not stupid.'

'I've never said you were.'

'You didn't need to say anything. I could tell we were worlds apart, but that made me all the more determined. I knew that my grandpa hadn't gone to all this trouble for me to produce a birth certificate. He wanted to make a better person of me and I'd like to think I rose to the occasion.'

'I admire you for that,' Melanie said. 'Lots of people would have taken the easy option. I would have taken the easy way out.'

'I know I had a one-to-one coach at the pool, but I did have to work at learning to swim. Once I'd achieved it and realised I could do it, that made me wonder what else I could do.'

'And so you taught yourself to read?'

'Not exactly,' Joe said. 'For years I've been doing a woman's garden. She was a teacher. One day I happened to tell her about the swimming and mentioned that I'd like to learn other things and she's helped me.'

Joe gestured to Melanie to sit and join him. She was still standing and hadn't touched her drink.

She sat and raised her glass.

'She must be a remarkable woman to get you to the point of reading aloud to an audience. I'm a confident reader but I don't like reading to other people.'

'She is a good teacher but I worked hard, too.' Joe grinned. 'She said I was her best pupil. I'd spend hours and hours practising my handwriting and slowly reading the newspaper from cover to cover. I didn't want Queenie or the men to know, so I rented her spare room.'

'Why didn't you want anyone to know?'

'They'd say I was getting ideas above my station, but I won't look back now.'

'You have done well, Joe,' Melanie said quietly as his words sunk in.

'Mrs Cooper, that's my teacher,' Joe continued, 'she's been promoted to head teacher. Part of the deal was that I would come to her school and do some oral storytelling, but as I became addicted to learning, she asked me to come and help some of her slower readers.

'I can't tell you how good it made me feel. I could really connect with those children. I've even started to help her son. You know, the one I told you about with Downs Syndrome?'

'The one you said could be your apprentice?'

'That's right. I can't believe I'm teaching him to read. Mrs Cooper said that's the best way for me to learn. I need to be able to understand it myself so I can show other people. I think it's the hardest thing I've ever had to do.'

'You did seem like a natural the day I came into school and saw you.'

'So, what were you doing there?'

'I'd just seen your van and wanted to suggest we meet for that drink but then I watched you reading and, well, I didn't know what to think.'

'Well, now you know. I wasn't proud

of myself when I first came into your office but, with Grandpa's help, I've come a long way. I think he'd be pleased.'

'I'm sure he would,' Melanie agreed as she raised her glass to Joe. 'And what's next on the agenda?'

'What do you mean?'

'Well, your grandfather's helped you open new doors. I wondered what other things you wanted to learn.'

'I can read a newspaper and understand my own bank statement. I still want to read a proper book. I haven't done that yet. I'm glad I've told you,' Joe added. 'I didn't want to say anything until the time was right.'

'And what's made you do it now?' Melanie asked. 'Oh, it's your next task, isn't it? Doing something brave, which could be telling me how you've grown from rags to riches?'

'Actually, I knew it was the right time because Mrs Cooper asked me if I wanted to study for an English exam.'

'Oh,' Melanie said. 'I didn't mean to belittle what you've done.'

'I'll admit,' Joe said, 'it hasn't been easy. I felt so useless in that Italian restaurant with you when I couldn't read the menu. I was ashamed.'

'But at least you did something about it.'

'I did, because I wanted your approval. I thought you might like me better if you felt I was more your equal.'

'Oh.'

'I'm sorry,' Joe said quickly.

He finished his glass of wine and poured another one.

'I didn't mean to be embarrassing. Tell me how you're getting on with reconnecting with your other family.'

Melanie finished her wine. She was glad Joe had moved the conversation on.

'It's not going very well. She's just a stranger to me. Sometimes I can hardly understand what she's saying and we haven't really found any common ground. In some ways I wish I'd never got in touch.'

'Is that why you've seemed a bit down lately?'

'Have I?'

Joe nodded.

'One minute you seem friendly and I think you like me, and then you've been irritable and quiet and I wonder if I've done something wrong.'

'I think something's going on at work,' Melanie said. 'Don't say anything to my mum, I don't want to worry her, but I think the company might be in financial trouble.'

'Are you sure? I mean you always seem so busy and it doesn't look as though you're over-spending. Mr Darcy certainly doesn't drive a sports car or take lots of holidays abroad.'

'No, neither of them are at all extravagant. I don't have any real evidence, but there have been a lot of whisperings going on and the other day the diary said that both brothers were in court all day, but they weren't. I think they'd gone to see their accountant.'

'That doesn't necessarily mean anything is wrong.'

'I suppose not, but there's been an

awkward atmosphere and two men did come and look at the building the other day. They then had a long meeting with both the brothers and nothing was in the diary to say who these men were.'

A Startling Revelation

Melanie helped her mum put away all her summer clothes at the weekend and get her winter jumpers out of the suitcases. She hung the heavy coats on the hangers and put her boots at the bottom of the wardrobe.

'All neat and tidy,' Melanie said as she showed her mother.

'Thank you so much for your help,' June said. 'I've made a cup of tea and there's something I wanted to show you. I found it at the bottom of a suitcase.'

Over their pot of tea, June showed Melanie a handwritten family tree.

'I remember doing this when we first adopted you. The social workers didn't tell us very much but I wanted to remember what they had said, just in case you ever asked.'

June slid the faded piece of paper

across the table in her direction. Melanie studied it for a few minutes and then looked up.

'I thought I was from Ireland,' she said at last.

'Your parents were, and you were born there, but they came over to London, and for whatever reason, could no longer care for you properly and that's when we had you.'

'So, do you think they went back to Ireland or stayed in London?'

'I've no idea. But I do remember the social worker saying that if you did ever want to get in touch, then you could let social services know, and they would look into the case.'

Melanie looked again at the family tree. There was a Bridget and there were members of the O'Mally family, but she was sure now there had been some mistake and the woman she'd been talking to on Skype was not her mother, after all. She felt relieved. She hoped the Bridget O'Mally she had spoken to wouldn't be too upset.

'I have started wondering about my other parents,' Melanie said firmly, 'so I think I should try to contact them, then at least I'll have some answers.'

⋆　⋆　⋆

First thing on Monday morning Melanie contacted social services to set the wheels in motion to find her parents. It took a few calls before she reached the right department but at least she felt she had done the right thing.

When Joe walked into the office later Melanie was able to see him for what he was. Joe Davies was a handsome, confident young man. He was a successful businessman and one who didn't give up very easily.

She knew she had learned from him. She was determined to see things to the end now and it was thanks to him.

'Good morning,' she said with a smile. 'Mr Darcy is in his office. You can go straight through.'

'Are you coming in, too?' he asked.

Melanie looked over at Anita but she nodded and waved the file at Melanie.

Anita had been busy on the phone all morning. Melanie had caught a little of the conversation but only enough to know that she'd been trying to organise an event. It sounded quite important.

'So,' Peter Darcy said, rising from his desk to greet Joe Davies like an old friend, 'not a year has passed and we're on to the final test set by your grandfather.'

He opened the envelope and read it out.

'This was something very dear to his heart and I think all your tasks so far have been preparing you for this. He wants you to build bridges between the two communities, the travellers and the goujo — the non-travellers, the house dwellers.'

'Joe has made a good start with this,' Melanie said and she told Mr Darcy about his work in schools.

'Have you ever thought about going into a high school or secondary school and giving an inspirational speech?'

'You sound just like Mrs Cooper, my teacher,' Joe said with a broad grin. 'She wants me to go to the local school to do their prize-giving and to tell them you're never too old to learn a new skill.'

'I'm sure your grandfather would be very proud of you if he were here today,' Mr Darcy said.

'I wish I'd known him,' Joe said. 'Why didn't he make contact?'

'In the early years he was grieving for his wife — your grandmother. He'd agreed Queenie should bring up his daughter Annie — that's your mother — and he paid her a monthly salary for doing so, but he worked abroad and didn't have much contact and then, of course, she was killed in the fire.'

'But he could have made contact with me!' Joe said.

'He didn't know you'd survived the fire. He came to his daughter's funeral but no-one spoke to him and if you read the newspaper reports at the time it focused on the lives lost rather than those saved.'

'When did he learn he had a grandson?'

'When he retired he was keen to get everything in order. He felt indebted to Queenie for being a good sister to his wife and for bringing up his daughter. He wanted to make sure she was comfortable in her old age. I suppose he felt she was the nearest thing he had to family.'

'She never told me any of this,' Joe said.

'It was only when he visited Queenie that he learned that you'd survived, but by this time he knew he was ill. He offered Queenie a house to live in, but she refused.'

★　★　★

The following morning Melanie came into the office and found a large pink envelope on her desk. It was an invitation to a meal on Friday to celebrate Anita's sixtieth birthday.

'Please say you can come,' Anita said as Melanie tore open the card. 'I've invited your mum, too.'

'That would be lovely,' Melanie said. 'But does this mean you are going to retire?'

'It does, and I need to talk to you about that, but can we leave it until Friday?'

The office was a hive of activity all day. Anita was in and out of the partners' offices and busy making phone calls.

Melanie was aware that some of it was of a personal nature and to do with her birthday party but she was conscious there were lots of other things going on and she didn't seem to be included in any of it.

Melanie was pleased when Joe called in to tell her that Nancy had been in touch with Queenie. They had made their peace and Nancy had offered to take her out for the day to meet Tara and her children.

'That's great news, Joe,' Melanie told

him. 'I bet you're pleased you went and spoke to her now.'

'Of course I am,' he said. 'But now they're trying to marry me off again. Nancy's second cousin was widowed recently and has two young children so now they're trying to match us up.'

'And how do you feel about that?' Melanie asked, but before Joe had a chance to answer Anita appeared and engaged him in conversation about her birthday on Friday.

Soon after that Peter Darcy summoned Melanie in to his office. He handed over a pile of files to be stored.

'May I ask you something?' Melanie said.

'You can ask,' Mr Darcy agreed. 'But I cannot guarantee an answer.'

'Why have things changed?' she asked. 'I mean, I used to be allowed to sit in on Joe's meetings but then you asked for Anita instead. I want to know why.'

Peter Darcy sat back in his chair.

'It was when Joe was asked to make a sacrifice that it all started,' he began.

217

'You may recall he asked for a private word?'

'Yes. What was that all about?'

'According to Joe he was making a huge sacrifice. He was very taken with you but felt you were, I think he said, 'out of his league'.'

'And what did you say?' Melanie probed.

'I said we all had to start somewhere. He may have lacked some skills but he ran a successful business. You may well have spent a few years at university but I could tell him you still had a lot to learn.'

'Thanks!'

'Well, in my opinion, it's true,' Mr Darcy said.

Melanie knew it was but as the saying went, the truth could hurt.

'Was he saying that he'd achieved that goal by not pursuing me? Is that what you mean?'

'That's what his argument was, but I wasn't having any of it and I told him so. It seems he took my advice.'

A Day to Remember

Most of the mail on Friday was for Anita, but hidden amongst it was a letter for Melanie. It was a large white envelope with a typewritten label.

Inside was a brief note from social services saying they had made contact with her birth parents and her mother had written to them immediately to give her permission for her details to be sent on.

They were forwarding the letter to her in case she wanted to make contact.

It was now up to her.

The enclosed letter was written on flowery notepaper.

Carefully, Melanie prised open the envelope. There was just one page of beautiful handwriting.

It was from her mother and father, both alive and well and living about 100 miles away.

I'm sure you have lots of questions to ask. Not least why we had you adopted. Your father and I would be delighted to meet with you and answer your queries.

Perhaps you'd like to suggest a date, time and place?

It's the least we can do.

Inside the envelope were a couple of old photographs. One was of Melanie as a baby and there was also one of her parents.

She liked the look of them and decided to give them a call at the first opportunity. The most important thing was that these pictures matched the ones June had given her the other day.

Now she knew for sure she'd found the right couple.

⋆　⋆　⋆

Anita and Melanie walked to work together as usual but were surprised to find both David and Peter Darcy already in the office on their arrival.

'Will you both come into the back

office before we open up?' Peter said.

Melanie assumed they had a birthday gift for Anita. She hung up her coat and left her bag near her desk and followed them all into the little back room.

'Do sit down,' David said formally.

He fidgeted and shuffled with some papers before Peter took over.

'It's big day, not just for you, Anita, but for Darcy and Darcy Solicitors.'

He paused and Melanie sat up a little bit straighter, her brain starting to work overtime.

'David and I have given this a great deal of thought and now seemed to be the right time. We have decided to merge our company with Watsons and . . . '

'Watsons?' Melanie gasped.

They were a huge national company with solicitors in most of the larger towns around the country. They mainly dealt with the buying and selling of houses and so most of their offices were based within estate agent offices.

It was definitely not the small family business with the scope for a wide variety of cases that Melanie had signed up for.

'Watsons have agreed to take on any existing staff,' Peter Darcy continued, 'but it will involve relocation as we have let this building with effect from the end of next month.'

'But that doesn't give me much notice,' Melanie said.

'One of the directors from Watsons is due in later this morning to sign some papers. He said he'd be delighted to talk to you.'

Melanie looked around her at her work colleagues.

She knew Anita had been talking of retiring.

She wasn't sure exactly how old either Peter or David were, but they were probably considering retirement, too.

'Is it only me this affects?' she asked.

There was a long silence and then Peter nodded.

'Anita and I are retiring. David and his wife, Eva, are moving to the coast where they are going to open a studio and art gallery. So yes, it does only affect you.'

'How long have you known about this?' Melanie asked.

'There have been a lot of discussions and obviously we couldn't say anything until decisions had been made which was only last month.'

'So you've known for at least a month and haven't said a word to me.'

'We were not in a position to disclose anything until certain papers were signed. I understand this has probably come as a bit of a surprise, Melanie, but I would advise you not to say anything until you've listened to what the gentleman from Watsons has to say.'

'And if I don't want to work for them?'

'You've only been with us a short time,' Peter Darcy began. 'We will pay you a month's salary and release you early if you find new employment before then. You have accrued some holiday.

'I think it will add up to a generous package but I would urge you to

223

consider what Watsons can offer you. They're a big company and can give you more training opportunities than we ever could.'

'But in a very narrow field of work.'

'Everyone has to start somewhere,' Peter Darcy said. 'We will, of course, give you a good reference wherever you decide to go.'

Melanie shook her head. There was so much to take in.

She was still coming to terms with the letter she'd received out of the blue that morning from her mother.

'May I go and get some fresh air?' she asked. 'There's such a lot to think about. I'll go and get a coffee and sit down for a while.'

'Half an hour at the most,' Peter Darcy said. 'I want you back in the office when the man from Watsons comes in. It's important you hear what he has to say.'

Melanie grabbed her bag and rushed across the road to the café where she'd first gone with Joe all those months ago.

Rather than immediately return to the office, she hurried along the high street to the park and soon found an empty bench. She pulled her jacket around her and looked at her phone.

Who should she call? Her first thought was to ring her mother but she didn't want to worry her.

She would wait until after she'd seen the man from Watsons, although she already knew it would mean moving away and then she wouldn't be in a position to care for her mother, so that was unlikely to be an option.

She had often turned to Anita for advice but today she was angry and hurt that no-one had confided in her. She understood that Anita may not have been at liberty to say anything, but that didn't make her feel any better.

Instead, she turned to her friend, Joe. He answered straightaway.

In her turmoil Melanie told him Darcys were closing and she would either have to move away to work for Watsons or find another job so she could stay locally and continue to care for her mother.

'And there's more,' she said breathlessly. 'I had a letter from my real parents and they've suggested we meet and they'll answer my questions.'

'I could meet you for lunch?' Joe suggested. 'I don't know that I can do anything but listen — but I could take your mind off things for an hour.'

'That's so kind, Joe, but I don't know when the man from Watsons is coming.'

She sighed as she remembered Anita's birthday meal that evening.

'I wish I hadn't said I was going.'

'If you play your cards right you could come out well from all this,' Joe said.

'Maybe, but at the moment it all seems like a lot of hassle.'

'Text me if there are any developments,' Joe said. 'I'll keep my phone on just in case you need to call me. I'll keep checking it because I don't always hear it when I'm mowing the lawn.'

'Thanks, Joe.'

She checked the time but decided she could make one more quick call. She rang the recruitment agency who had contacted her a short while ago.

'I may be looking for a new job after all,' she said. 'Do you have anything I might be interested in?'

'Leave it with me,' the man said. 'I'll check your CV and see what matches we have and e-mail you later.'

Melanie walked back to the office just as the man from Watsons arrived. He had a meeting with the Darcy brothers and signed some papers and then called her into the back office.

By this time Melanie had given her situation a bit more thought and was ready to negotiate.

More Surprises to Come

Melanie had her meeting. Watsons would offer her a job with good prospects and a slightly better salary, but not locally. She explained that she had family commitments and would have to give it some thought.

She was relieved when both the Darcy brothers and the man from Watsons all went out for a late working lunch.

'I would have spoken to you if I could,' Anita said, 'but I'd been asked to keep it confidential until they'd done the deal.'

'I do understand,' Melanie said, 'but it has come as a big shock to me.'

Anita took a deep breath and came and sat down near Melanie's desk.

'There's no easy way to say this,' she began and Melanie's heart sank.

What else could be happening now?

'I've decided to put the old house on the market. I'm going to buy something brand new which is easier to manage. You know, better than most, that it could be many months before the house sells. You're welcome to stay until then.'

Melanie fought back the tears but her eyes welled up.

'So, today I have learned that I'm losing my job and now you tell me that I'll have to find new accommodation?'

'I'm sure you wouldn't have wanted to stay in my spare room for much longer, anyway,' Anita told her. 'I don't know what Watsons offered you, but if you did want to take them up on it, I could help keep an eye on your mother. I may be moving house, but I'm going to stay in the area.'

Melanie wiped away a tear. She hadn't expected Anita to come up with a solution and was grateful for the offer.

'That's kind and I appreciate it but I need a bit of time to consider my options.'

'Of course.'

It was an odd sort of day. Melanie knew she ought to be getting on with her workload but her heart was no longer in it. There were only two more house sales she was involved in and both were due to exchange the following week.

She was glad that Anita suggested they close up early. Melanie hurried over to see her mum. She had taken her change of clothes and was going to get ready there and then head off for the restaurant together.

As she walked towards her mother's apartment her phone buzzed. It was the recruitment agency alerting her to an email they had just sent.

Melanie read it through and for the first time that day she began to feel a bit more cheerful. This particular job seemed much more interesting, paid considerably better and had far more promotion opportunities. The only downside was that it too would mean moving away, but not too far.

Melanie ran through the events of the day with her mother.

'You mustn't worry about me,' June said. 'I love having your company each day but it does make me lazy. If Mr Picard can manage to get to the corner shop every day then I'm sure I can.'

'Anita said she'd be happy to visit you most days.'

'That's very kind of her, she's a good sort.'

Joe had said things could actually work out to Melanie's advantage and perhaps they would, she thought.

She texted the recruitment agency and despite it being Friday evening they responded almost immediately saying they could set up an interview for Monday. Melanie agreed, and then got ready for Anita's birthday meal.

Although Melanie was feeling happier than she had done earlier in the day, she was still not looking forward to the evening.

Despite her reservations, the meal was delicious and no-one discussed work at all.

'Did you see that?' June whispered to her daughter.

'See what?' Melanie asked.

'Look at the way he's looking at Anita.' June gestured towards Peter Darcy.

Melanie could see what her mother was getting at.

'He often rings in the evenings,' Melanie said, 'but I always thought it was just about work.'

'Come to think of it,' June said, 'his name did keep coming into the conversation while we were away. I think they'd make a nice couple.'

'I did wonder what he was going to do once he'd retired. Other than read the odd crime novel, he only ever seems to spend his time working.'

'I'll have a little word with her when I get a chance,' June said with a sparkle in her eye.

★　★　★

Melanie had a successful interview and was offered a new job, so she could decline Watsons' offer. Once the two house sales had gone through she spoke to Peter Darcy who released her from her employment.

'Joe Davies is giving his inspirational talk to the sixth-form college this afternoon. I wondered if you wanted to go along?'

'I'd love to,' Melanie said quickly. 'I wanted to have a chance to say goodbye before I move away.'

'He'll be sorry to see you go,' Peter said. 'I must admit I had my reservations when Robert Huntley made his will but he's proved me wrong and the lad has exceeded expectations.'

* * *

Melanie sat at the back of the hall and listened as Joe talked. He started by telling everyone about his background and how he came from gypsy stock but just like any race or culture, there are people who you would be proud of, and those who give their fellows a bad name.

He went on to explain how he started

up in business and relied on others to do his accounts and promote his gardening work. He explained that his grandpa had set him different challenges and one was to produce a certificate.

So, he'd learned to swim and once he'd realised he could achieve something like that he got the bug for learning.

He spoke fluently, without notes, as though he was telling one of his oral traditional stories.

'The lightbulb moment,' he said, 'was when I met someone, a lady, and for the first time I felt that if I was ever going to be the sort of man who could win a girl like that and be able to provide for her, I would need to be able to read better. I didn't want to spend the rest of my life finding ways round my problem or making excuses.

'Not only that, but if one day I could have children of my own, I'd want to be able to read them stories and make sure they were proud of me.'

Melanie was so absorbed in his speech she didn't want it to end. She clapped along with everyone else and they gave him a standing ovation. She didn't move when everyone else started to leave the hall.

Joe was surrounded by people, all wanting to shake his hand or to thank him personally for sharing his story.

She knew she could go back to Peter Darcy and say she'd witnessed Joe Davies building bridges between the traveller community and the wider world. Nothing was going to change overnight, but at least these college students might not be so quick to judge in future.

Eventually the hall began to empty and Melanie moved forward. She needed to say goodbye but didn't want an audience.

'Hello,' Joe greeted her warmly. 'I thought I saw you at the back of the hall. I'm glad I didn't hear you snoring!'

'You did a good job,' Melanie told

him. 'You had them all captivated.'

'It seemed to go well,' he agreed.

'Any chance we could have a quiet chat?' she asked.

'Of course,' Joe said, glancing at his watch. 'But the primary school next door are just about to finish, and I'd love to pop in and see the children. You're welcome to join me.'

Melanie trailed along as Joe headed to the school playground. As soon as he was spotted he was surrounded by small children eager to talk to him.

'Joe, Joe!' they called.

They wanted to know when he was next coming in to tell them stories or to run the gardening club or to help them read.

Melanie stood back and watched. She not only saw the handsome man who'd become her friend but a warm and gentle giant who was so good with children. She realised that if she wasn't careful she'd fall in love with him.

It dawned on Melanie that although she'd come here to say goodbye, that wasn't what she wanted to do at all.

Joe had given her many opportunities to develop their friendship but she'd held him at arms' length and now she realised what a mistake she'd made. It was too late.

This had nothing to do with the fact she was moving away.

It was all to do with his grandpa.

Joe had now completed all twelve tasks. That meant he'd soon be inheriting a property and a large sum of money. If Melanie now, all of a sudden, showed a romantic interest in Joe, it would smack of her just being after his wealth.

She turned and slipped away before anyone could prevent her.

★   ★   ★

She couldn't get Joe out of her mind. She now knew that she'd already fallen for him, but couldn't see any way out of the situation. What was more, she knew it was inevitable that he'd come into the office in order to claim his prize.

She was well aware Peter Darcy was expecting him and that there was a large bottle of champagne chilling in the fridge with which to celebrate his achievement.

Together For Ever

True to form, Joe arrived the following day. He smiled at Melanie and approached her desk.

'You disappeared,' he said. 'I tried to phone but you were on voicemail. At least you'll be able to get on with your work now and I won't keep coming in and bothering you,' he teased.

'I've got a new job to go to,' Melanie told him. 'I'm moving away.'

'But what about your mother?' Joe asked. 'You can't leave her.'

'It's all sorted. I won't be too far away.'

Peter Darcy had obviously heard his voice and came into the room.

'I thought it was you.' He held out his hand. 'Congratulations are in order, I believe.'

'Thank you, sir. And thank you for all your help and support.'

'Come into the office. I've sorted out some old photos I found of your grandfather, I thought you might like them.' Darcy turned to Melanie. 'Can you bring in the champagne?'

The two men disappeared into Peter's office. Melanie set the tray and took in the bottle and two glasses.

'I think we're all entitled to a glass,' Peter said. 'It's been quite a team effort. Can you fetch a couple more glasses and bring Anita in, too?'

Melanie disappeared back into the main office and the kitchen area.

'He wants us to join them in his office. Joe's completed the last of the tasks.'

Anita looked up and smiled.

'I hope you're going to stay in touch with him,' she said.

'I can't.'

'Why not?'

'Up until now I've always tried to be professional. I've played it cool and not let myself get involved.'

'And that's very commendable, but

240

you're leaving the company now and so it doesn't matter any more. We've all become fond of Joe. He's like family.'

'But if I now tell him what I feel for him, he'll think I'm just after his money,' Melanie said.

'No, I won't,' a voice said from behind her. 'I couldn't help hearing what you said. Peter sent me to see what was keeping you both.'

'Oh,' Melanie said.

Anita took the extra glasses and headed for Peter's office, leaving the two of them together in the kitchen.

'So, tell me,' Joe said, 'what is it that you feel about me?'

Melanie blushed. She didn't know how to tell him how she felt.

'You heard my speech,' Joe said. 'I told everyone how I'd met this lady — you — and how I felt about her and the lengths I went to so that I would feel worthy of her and that one day I'd be able to provide for her.

'Well, now I've got a house. I'm hoping to persuade Queenie to come and live with me there. You do realise that although I may have changed in many ways, family is, and always will be, my priority.'

'I know that.'

'I've only seen pictures of the property so far but I'd be really grateful if you'd come and have a look at it with me.'

'Me?'

'Yes. I need to know what you think about it. I want to know if you could picture yourself living there one day, with me, with Queenie and, if we're blessed, with children of our own.'

'Oh, Joe, do you mean it?'

In answer, Joe scooped her up into his arms and gently kissed her. In the background they heard the pop of the champagne cork. There was much to celebrate.

A Special Meeting

Melanie asked Joe to accompany her when she went to meet her 'real' parents.

Bridget O'Mally was a warm woman with a big smile. She greeted Melanie and Joe like old friends.

'Come in. John's by the fire,' she said, leading the way.

John O'Mally had twinkling blue eyes, not unlike Joe. He sat in a wheelchair with a tartan rug over his lap and smiled when they entered the room.

Bridget poured them tea and offered round her homemade lemon cake. Melanie couldn't help notice how tenderly Bridget looked after her husband.

'She looks like . . . you,' John said slowly to his wife and Bridget smiled proudly.

'I know you must have a lot of questions,' Bridget said quietly to Melanie.

'Well, the most important thing is, why? Why was I adopted in the first place?'

Bridget looked at John. She reached over and stroked his arm.

'We'd been married a year and had a nice little house on the outskirts of London. We were so looking forward to having our baby, but John had been having a couple of funny turns. He was dizzy and couldn't always see properly. We knew something was wrong, although we had no idea how bad it was. Just before you were born he was diagnosed with multiple sclerosis.

'We were devastated, of course, but we loved each other and there was the baby to look forward to.'

John gave a lop-sided smile.

'Even though we knew the baby was due, we had to go home to see our families. We returned to Ireland and you were born there.' Bridget sipped her tea and then carried on.

'After a couple of weeks we travelled back to London with our new baby but

John was deteriorating and we both knew it was only going to get worse. John had been a teacher and the school were very good, but it soon became apparent, because his speech sounded so slurred, that he wasn't going to be able to carry on.'

'Before you were born,' Bridget said, 'I was a nurse. We were both realistic. We knew John wasn't going to be able to work for much longer. He was getting weaker with each week.

'I did my best, but I couldn't manage a new baby, a job and caring for John. Something had to give.'

John looked at Bridget. He nodded as if giving her permission to go on.

'John felt awful. He was filled with guilt, although of course he'd never done anything wrong. It was just one of those dreadful things.

We agreed we wanted the best for our daughter and we decided that if we found a loving couple who couldn't have children of their own, then they would be able to give you a proper family life, something we knew we'd not be able to do.'

Bridget wiped away a tear.

'It was the hardest thing we ever did but even now, I know we made the right decision. Look at you!'

She squeezed Melanie's hand.

'What a wonderful girl you've turned into. I was right to pester that social worker so she got the best people. How are they?'

'I've lost my dad, but Mum's fine and yes, you couldn't have picked a more loving pair.' Melanie hugged Bridget.

'But I haven't finished the story,' Bridget said. 'Not long after we handed you over, John's condition stabilised. We had a good few years. By then you would have been settled and we felt it was best not to interfere. We considered ourselves lucky and now, here we are, reunited and thrilled to be invited to your wedding!'

Three Years Later

Melanie looked at the tête-à-tête daffodils Joe had given her. She couldn't believe how well everything had turned out.

Here she was, living in a beautiful home out in the countryside, surrounded by those she loved.

The house was big enough for Queenie to have had her own room but she'd chosen a mobile home which was now situated at the bottom of the garden hidden by a row of conifers, giving her some privacy and a little garden of her own.

June had had both knees operated on and was able to keep up with her grandchildren, Mary, two, and Robbie, who was just a year old and crawling everywhere.

David and Eva visited often, as did Anita and Peter. Eva had done a set of paintings of their home, one for each season.

Melanie looked from the winter scene and then to her favourite one with the purple crocuses on the front lawn.

She looked at the clock. Everything was ready.

Joe and his cousin had worked hard to adapt the old stable block into a granny annexe especially designed for when Bridget and John came to stay.

Joe appeared with Mary in one hand and Robbie in the other and gave her one of his winning smiles just as Bridget drove through the gates with John by her side.

We do hope that you have enjoyed reading this large print book.

Did you know that all of our titles are available for purchase?

We publish a wide range of high quality large print books including:
Romances, Mysteries, Classics
General Fiction
Non Fiction and Westerns

Special interest titles available in large print are:
The Little Oxford Dictionary
Music Book, Song Book
Hymn Book, Service Book

Also available from us courtesy of Oxford University Press:
Young Readers' Dictionary
(large print edition)
Young Readers' Thesaurus
(large print edition)

For further information or a free brochure, please contact us at:
Ulverscroft Large Print Books Ltd.,
The Green, Bradgate Road, Anstey,
Leicester, LE7 7FU, England.
Tel: (00 44) **0116 236 4325**
Fax: (00 44) **0116 234 0205**

THE LOCKET OF LOGAN HALL

Christina Garbutt

Newly widowed Emily believes she will never love again. Working as an assistant in flirtatious Cameron's antiques shop, she finds a romantic keepsake in an old writing desk. Emily and Cameron set off on a hunt for the original owner, and the discoveries they make on the way change both of them forever. But Emily doesn't realise that Cameron is slowly falling in love with her. Is his love doomed to be unrequited, or will Emily see what's right in front of her — before it's too late?